As I came to the garden I could see Kel in his backyard cleaning a gun with some brushes and old rags. Pale spring sunlight gleamed on his hair. He didn't even turn around. I let out a tiny sigh as I put down my tray of seedlings. Then all at once, I saw that the seedlings that I had just planted the day before had vanished. I caught my breath sharply, feeling a little dizzy. What was going on here anyway? I had planted them so carefully and now they were gone!

JANICE HARRELL lives with her husband and young daughter in a cedar-shingled house on a pond in North Carolina. She can look up from her typewriter and see a heron taking off from the pond or watch a monarch butterfly sipping from her zinnias. She tends to write the kind of story she likes to read—a funny story.

Dear Readers:

Thank you for your many enthusiastic and helpful letters. In the months ahead we will be responding to your suggestions. Just as you have requested, we will be giving you more First Loves from the boy's point of view; and for you younger teens, younger characters. We will be featuring more contemporary, stronger heroines, and will be publishing, again in response to your wishes, more stories with bittersweet endings. Since most of you wanted to know more about our authors, from now on we will be including a short author's biography in the front of every First Love.

For our Book Club members we are publishing a monthly newsletter to keep you abreast of First Love plans and to share inside information about our authors and titles. These are just a few of the exciting ideas that First Love from Silhouette has in store for you.

Nancy Jackson
Senior Editor
Silhouette Books

SECRETS IN
THE GARDEN
Janice Harrell

First Love from Silhouette
Published by Silhouette Books New York
America's Publisher of Contemporary Romance

First Love from Silhouette by Janice Harrell

Puppy Love #67
Heavens to Bitsy #95
Secrets in the Garden #128

SILHOUETTE BOOKS,
300 E. 42nd St., New York, N.Y. 10017

Copyright © 1985 by Janice F. Harrell
Cover photograph copyright © 1985 Bill Charles

Distributed by Pocket Books

ISBN: 0-373-06003-3

First Silhouette Books printing February, 1985

10 9 8 7 6 5 4 3 2 1

America's Publisher of Contemporary Romance

Printed in the U.S.A.

RL 5.8, IL age 11 and up

SECRETS IN
THE GARDEN

1

I was probably the very first person to see Kel Reid when he came to town. That was because his family moved in right next door to us. The Harrisons' house had been up for sale for a year, and we had just about decided that nobody was nutty enough to buy it. Then one day when I was propped up on elbows at the front window watching the birds with my binoculars, a moving van pulled up next door. It's quite a distance from our window to the road out front and what with the hedge, it wasn't easy for me to see what was going on next door. But a moving van is a pretty big item. Also, I had the binoculars.

"Good grief!" I said. "It's a moving van at the Harrisons'!"

My little brother Tim snatched the binoculars from me. "Wow!" he said. "Somebody's moving in all right."

I could make out the driver climbing down from the cab

of the truck and looking at the house. He scratched his head. Probably he couldn't believe he had the right address. The house has looked pretty strange ever since the Harrisons put in the carillon tower and the stained glass windows in front.

A little blue Mazda had pulled in ahead of the van and a boy got out from the driver's side. He seemed to be telling the mover that this was the right place. I grabbed the binoculars back from Tim to get a better look at him. He was a tall boy, wearing a fur-lined suede jacket and jeans. I adjusted the focus and got a very good close-up of his face. I could see he had slicked-down dark blond hair and a straight nose. Suddenly he turned and looked directly at me with steady blue eyes. It shook me so much I dropped the binoculars. I knew he probably couldn't see me from where he was, but it was unnerving just the same.

Mom picked up the binoculars and took a look herself. "I can't believe somebody's finally bought the place," she said.

"I think it's pretty pathetic," Dad said, "when the only thing the family can think of to do on a Saturday morning is spy on the neighbors."

"Goodness, George," Mom said, fiddling with the focus, "they're unloading guns."

Dad snatched the binoculars from her without ceremony. He screwed up his eyes and scrutinized the movers carefully. Standing behind him I couldn't see very well, but it looked to me as if they were unloading a big, glass-fronted case. Sunlight glanced off the glass front of it as they loaded it onto a dolly.

"They must collect guns," Dad said, trying to sound unconcerned. "It's not such an unusual hobby."

Dad had always said that the next neighbors *had* to be better than the crazy Harrisons with their wild parties, but so far our first look at the Reids wasn't reassuring. It looked as if they were planning the violent overthrow of the government. Now I could see the movers were bringing a second glass-fronted case out of the van.

Mom stood up. "You're right, George," she said. "It's silly for us to sit here glued to the window. We have better things to do. Tim, I'm going to be checking on your room in one hour flat. If it's not clean, no television. Corrie, I could use some help with lunch."

So Tim and I had to move away from the window. I reluctantly trailed Mom into the kitchen. I noticed, though, that Dad was in no rush to tear himself away. He was still peering anxiously through the binoculars when we left.

"I feel so sorry for the kids in that family," Mom said as she opened the refrigerator and got the celery out, "moving in the middle of the school year."

I thought of the cool gaze of the boy I had seen through the binoculars. "The one I saw didn't look exactly pitiful to me," I said.

Mom pulled the chicken out of the fridge. "Just the same," she said, "before Christmas is no time for a family to be moving. Now, Corrie, this time, please slice just the celery, not your fingers. Okay?"

Making chicken salad is, to put it mildly, not my favorite thing. Luckily it's something a person can do with

9

half a mind, and soon even though my fingers were slicing celery, the important part of me was far away, dreaming about the upcoming Christmas party. I like any sort of party, but this one was going to be special, a grown-up dance that several families had gotten together to give. It wasn't going to be held in the gym with tumbling mats rolled up in the corner and tissue-paper flowers hanging from the basketball hoops. This dance was going to be lovely and elegant. I could already feel myself floating along the dance floor, all the world aglitter, like in old movies, my shimmery dress swinging softly around me.

"Corrie," said Mom sharply. "Do watch what you're doing."

I came to with a start.

"Honestly," Mom said. "It continues to amaze me how a clever girl like you can mess up something as simple as slicing celery."

I saw guiltily that the celery, instead of being in neat, bite-sized pieces, was in great hunks held together by green strings of celery. "Sorry," I said.

It's never been very clear to me how people keep their minds on celery. I mean, what could be more boring? The minute I look at a celery stalk my mind goes blank. I wished Mom would just give up asking me to help out around the house, but she seemed to be determined to teach me what she called "basic survival skills." Mom can do anything around the house, from getting ink out of a blouse to reshingling the roof. She's a practical kind of person and she's done her best to get me to be that way, too. She has already tried, with no luck, to teach me how to knit, how to clean air-conditioning filters, and how to put up curtains. The trouble is that, while I don't have a bit of difficulty remembering the capital of Idaho and can instantly figure the area of a triangle, everything Mom has tried to teach me about housekeeping vanishes instantly from my mind like smoke in the wind. That doesn't bother me. I'm pretty happy just the way I am. Not everyone can be practical and I'm not even sure I want to be. I've already decided that it would be nicer to spend my time working at something interesting and pay somebody else to do the housework.

I tried hard, though, to concentrate on the celery, slice by boring slice, and finally we got the chicken salad made and put away in the refrigerator. When we'd finished I went into the living room and took a peek out the front window again. There was no sign of the boy I had seen through the binoculars. The movers were still at work, but all they were unloading now were ordinary things like kitchen chairs. I didn't see how I could find out much about the new family from their kitchen chairs. It was too bad I'd had to leave when the interesting stuff was being brought out, I thought.

Of course, I didn't realize it then, but within a week I would be finding out everything I wanted to know about the new family. Almost right away Tim became best buddies with Jason Reid, and from that time on he practically lived over there. Every night for the next two weeks we were treated to breathless bulletins on the Reids while we ate dinner.

"Jason has his own rifle," Tim said one night, reaching for the mashed potatoes. "All the Reid kids have rifles. When can I have a rifle, huh, Dad?"

"Never," said Dad firmly.

"Aw, I never get to have any fun," complained Tim. "Boy, you should see the snake skin they've got hanging up on the garage. I bet it's six feet long. Kel got it with just one shot last week when they were out duck hunting."

Any normal family would spend the first week or two after they moved in doing things like hanging up pictures, but not the Reids. At their house nothing was ever allowed to interfere with the hunting season. There were five boys—Brad, who was in college and home only on the weekends; Kel, my age, whom I had seen with the binoculars the day they moved in; Marty, an eighth grader; Jason, Tim's friend, a sixth grader; and Bucky, who was eight. I don't think they had even finished unpacking before they all went duck hunting, even little Bucky.

I had seen Mrs. Reid a couple of times when she came out to the road to get the mail, and she didn't look like much of a match for the boys. She was a little woman with sloping shoulders and a sweet but worried expression. She was probably wondering what her kids were going to shoot or blow up next. I decided the boys must take after their father. I had seen him jogging in the morning and, with that iron jaw of his, he looked like a match for anybody.

Since the house next door had been empty so long, we had gotten used to having peace and quiet, but after the Reids came all that changed. Engines roared, people yelled, and doors slammed at all hours. Our house wasn't really very close to theirs, but we could hear them, all right. It was like living next door to a fireworks factory. I

12

noticed the Reids hadn't been living next to us very long before Mom quit saying she felt sorry for the kids and started saying she felt sorry for Mrs. Reid. One day Jason even exploded his chemistry set in the front yard. Naturally, I thought I'd better keep an eye on what was going on. I didn't want him to blow us up next. I got into the habit of keeping my binoculars by the window so as not to miss anything.

My friend Terri noticed the binoculars one day when she came over. "Do you always whip out those things every time one of them comes outside?" she asked.

"Pretty much," I said, focusing on Kel. He was pouring antifreeze into the Mazda.

"Let me have a look," said Terri, taking them from me. She peered at Kel a few minutes, then heaved a little sigh. "He really is good-looking," she said.

"Maybe," I said, "but he's not my type. All he's interested in is shooting wild animals. What they do to those poor little ducks makes my blood run cold. Believe me, Terri, those are weird people over there. Day before yesterday, Jason took his chemistry set out on the front lawn, and the next thing I knew it had exploded."

She looked at me wide-eyed. "Exploded? I never heard of a chemistry set doing that before."

"I think Jason added some things of his own to it," I said darkly.

"Well, they're cute boys, anyway," she said.

It wasn't the cuteness of the Reid boys that interested me. It was that they were so strange. They were so different from me that I just couldn't understand them. Why would they want to be sloshing through the winter mud when they could be curled up by the fire with a good book? How could they honestly like killing little animals? And why did they have to make such an incredible racket all day long? Didn't they ever crave some quiet so they could think? The Reids' house might be only next door, but as far as I was concerned it was another world.

I couldn't keep brooding over the weirdness of the Reid family all day, though. Terri and I had to get down to working on something important. She had come over to teach me how to French braid my hair for the Christmas party. I bent over near the fire and started brushing it out.

"Ready?" said Terri. She came to stand beside me and started trying to put my hair up into braids the way her cousin Lisa had shown her, but soon she was biting her lip. "I don't know," she said. "It looked so simple when Lisa was doing it. She didn't end up with all these little bits and pieces sticking out."

I held up the mirror to take a look. What I wanted to look like for the party was a medieval princess, and I figured that I needed a romantic, sleek look for my hair. From what I could see, I thought Terri and I were on the right track with the French braids. Somehow we just needed to get them smoothed up.

It was at times like this that I wished I had springy dark hair like Terri's. All she did on special occasions was stick a sprig of flowers in it and off she went. My hair, on the other hand, long, straight, and blond, was the ultimate "fill-in-the-blank" as far as hair went. It looked fantastic as long as I had an hour and a half to work on it. Otherwise, it looked very, very plain.

"Do you think we could get Lisa to come over here and give us some pointers?" I asked, eyeing the messy braids.

Terri sank into an armchair. "It's tricky, Corrie," she said. "I think it might take us a while to get the knack of it. Instead, maybe we should try to get her to come and braid it for you herself on the day of the party."

"Do you think she would?" I asked. "I would think up some way to pay her back."

Terri glanced at the window toward the Reids' house. "Maybe you could let her look through the binoculars at Kel," she said. "What a piece of luck that he moved in next door to you."

"Not exactly luck," I said. I had thought about it in the past couple of weeks and I had realized that if the Reids hadn't bought that house somebody like them would have. It was the kind of house that could only be used by a big, wild family. After all, not just anybody can use a five-bedroom house with a bell tower. "They had to move there," I told Terri. "I'll bet that was the only house in Wolverton big enough to hold all of them and their guns."

"That's what I said," said Terri. "It had to happen. It's fate."

"More like doom," I said. I wondered why some thoughtful, kind boy couldn't have moved in next door, someone maybe who wrote poetry and had soulful dark eyes, deep and mysterious as a mountain pool.

"What did you ever do about your elective next semester?" Terri asked suddenly, shaking me out of my nice little daydream. It was easy for me to follow her train of thought. I had said "doom," so naturally she had thought of my problem with electives. There was no denying that for me electives equal doom. At our school you have to sign up for a certain number of them before you graduate, and that's the part of school that gives me nightmares. Unlike a lot of people, I happen to like chemistry, algebra, and English. I like them and I'm good at them. What was driving me crazy was picking out an elective. All of them were either practical or depressing. It was hard to say which I hated most—chorus, where they stood around singing awful songs like "You'll Never Walk Alone";- counseling, where people were encouraged to talk about their troubles; or home economics, where they still teach making beds. They were all terrible.

I looked around me furtively and lowered my voice. "I've signed up for general science," I said.

Terri looked puzzled. "But general science isn't an elective," she said.

"No," I said, "but I'm hoping no one will notice."

"Ooo, I think that's risky," said Terri. "What if they catch it next year when you're a senior and they stop you from graduating?"

Terri had a lot more faith in the efficiency of the staff of Wolverton High than I did. I was sure they would never catch it. They were always telling us how overworked the office staff was, weren't they? And it wasn't as if they would be expecting someone to try to sneak out of taking an elective. Also, general science was a perfectly legitimate course. It was what kids who weren't going to college took instead of chemistry and physics. In it they explained how telephones work and taught you about what went on at the city sewage plant. I thought it sounded interesting. It was certainly more interesting than making beds, anyway.

"I don't think they'll catch me," I said.

"Ooo, it's risky," Terri repeated nervously. "Why don't you go in after Christmas and tell them you made a mistake and then register for home ec instead?"

I suppressed a shudder. "I'd be a disaster at home ec," I said. "I can't even pop popcorn without burning it."

"That's just because you don't keep your mind on it," said Terri. "Honest, home ec isn't so bad. Barbara had to take it, and she said they didn't get around to doing that much. Mrs. Johnson likes to give advice so much that there really isn't much time left for classwork. Barbara says she'll start out saying, 'Now, girls . . . ,' and before you know it she's been talking for half an hour about the joys of motherhood."

Barbara was Terri's big sister, and Terri always followed her advice to the letter.

"I still think I can get by with taking general science," I said.

"Well, maybe you're right," Terri said. "I guess I can't really imagine them telling somebody who has straight A's that she can't graduate because she didn't take home ec."

That was what I was counting on. All the same, I was a little nervous about the whole thing. I knew I was going to feel better when the holidays were over and I had actually started general science. I wanted to stop worrying about it. I looked at myself in the mirror. "How do you think it would look with maybe a thin silver ribbon braided in?" I asked.

That night I called Terri's cousin Lisa, and she said she'd be happy to come over and braid my hair for me the day of the party, but that she'd have to do it in the morning because she'd promised to take her grandmother Christmas shopping that afternoon. That was fine with me. If she'd said she had to come a whole day before, I would have just figured I'd have to sleep standing up so as not to mess up the braids. I really did want to look nice for the party.

Saturday morning Lisa came as she had promised and did my hair. The rest of the day I was careful not to go outside at all. I was afraid the wind would make those funny little pieces stick out all over and that I wouldn't know how to fix them.

I knew I was going to have a wonderful time at the party. I had blown my entire baby-sitting savings on my dress, and it was perfect—swingy, glittery, and soft. The only possible hitch in the evening was that I was going to the party with Marshall, who lives down the road from us. It was hard to say exactly why I had told Marshall I would go with him. I love to dance, and I did want to go to the party. But I think the real reason is that I have too much imagination. It wasn't hard for me to see what it would be like to ask a girl out. How utterly grim if, after you'd worked yourself up to it, she said no! So I said yes.

It wasn't as if there were anything actually wrong with Marshall. He was good-looking in a glitzy sort of way. And he wasn't dumb. The problem was that whenever I looked into his eyes I was reminded of dead fish, which is not the sort of thing that cheers a person up. And he wasn't easy to have a conversation with. He had a way of acting as if the last interesting thing that had happened was over before any of us was born.

But after all, I told myself, everything else about the party would be wonderful and beautiful, and probably Marshall wouldn't turn out to be so bad once I got to know him better.

Saturday evening he came by to pick me up at eight. We didn't have much to say to each other, but it was lovely to be driving off to a party, smelling nice from a bubble bath and feeling like a princess on her way to a ball. It was too bad, I thought, gently touching my dress, that life didn't have more of this kind of thing and less of making chicken salad.

The party was at Ralston House, a beautiful old mansion that the city rents out for things like wedding receptions. It was the kind of building I can really love, built in the days when dashing men rode on horseback and ladies in long dresses swept up the front flight of steps to balls. We made our way up the stairs to the mansion's front door and stepped inside into the party. A rush of warm air hit us, and I could hear a band playing. The room was filled with people dancing. A pretty woman floated by us, jewelry glittering in her upswept dark hair. I was glad I had blown my baby-sitting money on my dress. I wanted to look as if I belonged here. Marshall disappeared to go hang up our coats but was soon back. "Want some punch?" he asked. "Or want to dance?"

"I want to dance," I said. I could already feel the music calling to me. It seemed as close to me as my heartbeat. He took my hand and led me into the midst of the people dancing. There was quite a crowd, people of all ages. As we danced by the punch bowl, he said, "Looks like Mary Ellen has come without a date again."

Mary Ellen gave me a little wave as we went by. I felt uncomfortable. I hoped she hadn't heard Marshall talking about her. "Aren't the decorations beautiful," I said, looking for a safe subject.

He looked about us at the boughs of holly fixed to the cornices with red velvet bows. "Somebody sure laid out a bundle on them," he said.

When I finally realized that all I could expect from Marshall were unpleasant cracks about other people and guesses about how much the party was costing, I tried to concentrate on my dancing. I'm not one of those people who likes to have music playing around me all the time. It seems to tug at me, making me want to dance, and that would be confusing if I were trying to work algebra problems or wash my hair, for instance. But tonight having the music was heaven. While Marshall was being so sour I was able to lose myself in it.

Suddenly Terri and Joe bumped into us. Joe is a very unreliable navigator on the dance floor, and we hadn't seen him plunging toward us in time to get out of his way. I knew he must have done plenty of stepping on Terri's toes, but she looked happy. "Nice party, huh?" said Joe, his friendly face breaking into a grin. Then they swiftly danced away.

After a while the room, which had seemed so nicely warm when we came in, started to feel hot. "Why don't we get some punch?" I said. I was thirsty. Also, I was hoping we would run into somebody we knew at the punch bowl. I figured I could use a change from Marshall's conversation.

We edged our way through the crowded room to Mary Ellen at the punch bowl. The circle of ice floating in the punch bobbed as she dipped in the ladle to fill our cups. Marshall's eyes were busy scanning the dance floor. I tried to smile at Mary Ellen twice as hard in order to make up for Marshall ignoring her.

"Are you going to be in chorus next term?" she asked.

"I hope not," I said.

"What are you going to take then?" she asked.

I looked around to make sure no one else was listening and then whispered, "general science."

She looked puzzled. "But general science isn't an elective," she said.

"I'm hoping nobody will notice," I said.

Mary Ellen laughed. "Well, good luck," she said.

Marshall had finished his survey of the dance floor. "Ready to go again?" he said.

"Just let me have a cookie," I said, stalling. I wasn't quite willing yet to face talking to Marshall again.

All at once Kel Reid showed up next to us. Mary Ellen's round face immediately began to turn pink. "Hi, Kel," she said faintly. She stopped to clear her throat. "Do you know Corrie and Marshall?" she asked.

It really was exasperating to see the effect he had on people. I wondered a bit anxiously whether I was turning pink too. It was so unsettling to have him show up suddenly like that, not in boots and all spattered with mud the way I was used to seeing him in his backyard but looking smooth and well brushed. He looked at me steadily with those cool blue eyes. They were a light, clear color with dark lashes, and they seemed to look right through you, as if he were reading your thoughts. It was that very look that had made me drop the binoculars the day I first saw him, and when you came to think of it, it wasn't a very polite way of looking at a person. I would have loved to act as if I didn't notice him looking at me, but that was harder than I thought it would be.

"Corrie and I are neighbors," he said. He looked Marshall up and down, then smiled slightly. "And Marshall and I have met." There was something very uncomfortable about the way he said it, as if he knew all about Marshall's faults. He was somehow making me feel as if I should be ashamed of being out with Marshall. There was nothing I could do. I just stood there, frozen, hating Kel for making me feel so awful.

"Why don't you get somebody to take over the punch bowl so we can dance?" Kel asked Mary Ellen.

"Let them get their own punch," she said, promptly dropping the ladle.

He gave her his arm in the sort of old-fashioned gesture my father might make and led her off.

"That Kel Reid is so full of himself," said Marshall.

Actually, I agreed with Marshall about Kel but I didn't want to be pulled into making nasty remarks about everybody in sight. I took a deep breath and looked around me rather wildly. "I think they have a wonderful band tonight, don't you?" I said. As we danced away I caught a glimpse of myself in the mirror over the big, old-fashioned fireplace where two candles burned on the mantle. My face looked strangely unfamiliar framed by the braids. "What are you feeling so shattered about?" I asked myself. "What do you care what Kel Reid thinks about Marshall? Anyway, you aren't marrying Marshall, for heaven's sake. You're only going to a party with him."

Later that night, when Marshall drove me home, I had to listen to him talk about his upcoming ski trip. His family always spent Christmas skiing in Aspen, Colorado. It wouldn't be my idea of fun to spend Christmas in a hotel, no matter how fancy it was, but Marshall seemed to think it was great. As he started to go on and on about the new ski equipment he had bought I could see that he could talk about it for some time without any encouragment, so I let my mind wander. I found myself wondering what Kel did on Christmas. Went out and shot harmless little bunny rabbits probably. And how had he even gotten himself asked to the Christmas party anyway? You wouldn't have thought he'd had that much time to get to know people. Maybe he had given someone that icy look of his and they had invited him in sheer terror. Look at the way Mary Ellen had fallen apart at his glance. Pitiful.

The next afternoon Terri came over so we could rehash the party. "You looked gorgeous," she said. "The braids were great. It was really good we got Lisa to do them. I could never have gotten them to look like that."

"You looked great too," I said.

"Lucky thing Barbara and I are the same size," Terri said. "That was her dress. Oh, didn't you just love, love, love the party?"

"It was nice," I said, twisting my hair around a finger.

Terri looked at me in surprise. "Is that all you can say? Nice?"

"It would have been nicer if I hadn't been with Marshall," I said. "All night he kept making nasty cracks about everybody in sight."

"Just take it with a grain of salt," said Terri, dancing a few steps across the living room. "Concentrate on the music, the lovely, lovely people, the utter neatness of it all." She threw herself down on the couch.

I was pretty sure Terri would have thought it was a lot less neat if she had been with Marshall. "Why did I ever say I would go with Marshall anyway?" I said.

"It's because you feel sorry for people too easily," Terri said promptly.

"You think?"

"The original marshmallow heart," she said positively. "After all, have you ever told a boy you didn't want to go out with him?"

"I'm not asked out every day, you know," I hedged.

"I rest my case," said Terri.

"But usually only boys you like ask you out anyway," I said. "A boy can tell if you don't want to go out with him, so it doesn't mean anything that I've never said no."

Terri raised her finger. "What about Marshall?" she said.

I squirmed. "Well, maybe Marshall didn't quite realize yet that I don't much like him."

"You should have said no," said Terri smugly.

"I hated to hurt his feelings," I said. "I could see how he must have felt."

24

She gave me a look. "Oh, maybe you're right," I said. "Maybe I am too soft-hearted. I guess I ought to work on that."

"I wouldn't worry about it," said Terri. "Your marshmallow heart is saved from a boring smushiness by your ruthlessness about your grades."

"I don't think I'm all hung up about grades," I said, stung. "I may kind of like to be at the top of the class, but there's nothing wrong with that."

"I just think it's interesting," said Terri, "that Otis Boggs, your chief competition, is the only boy you never feel sorry for."

"Nobody could feel sorry for Otis," I said.

"You'd cut his throat to get ahead of him," said Terri.

"I would not."

"Ha," said Terri.

"I'm not sorry for Kel Reid either," I said quickly. "I'm not a bit sorry for him."

Terri grinned. "Maybe there's hope for you," she said, stretching out on the couch. "You know, people are so interesting. I never get tired of figuring them out. Maybe I'll be a psychologist someday."

"You'd need top grades for that," I said tartly. I wasn't altogether happy at the way she had analyzed my character.

Terri leaned over and peeked out the front window in the direction of the Reids' yard. "No sign of Kel," she said. "I guess he's inside."

I felt kind of low. First Kel had looked me up and down as if he were counting my shortcomings, and now Terri was telling me my whole personality could use some work. "I wish Kel would move away again," I burst out. "Now I'll never be able to get away from him and that superior look of his."

"Maybe he'll grow on you," said Terri.

I threw a pillow at her.

2

School started again on the third of January. I was one of the few people who was really glad. It hadn't been much fun for me helping Mom out around the house during vacation; it was always "Corrie, watch out!" and "Not *that* way," and half the time, "Where is your mind, Corrie?" One thing for sure, my mind was not on housework. I was looking forward to being in school again so I would be too busy to help out in the kitchen. Of course, the other thing was that I was anxious to start general science and prove to myself that I was going to get away with taking it.

General science was scheduled for third period, and I set off for Room 204 with all the confidence of a convict riding out through the prison gates in a laundry truck. I am a person who usually follows the rules, and even though I knew I wasn't exactly committing a crime and even though I had good reason to think I was going to get away with it, I was very nervous.

When I edged into the classroom, trying to look inconspicuous, I saw a lot of unfamiliar faces. I knew some of the kids from home room and from the ninth grade, but the way my school is set up, I normally don't see much of those kids who are planning to join their dads on the tobacco farm after graduation or who are studying to be hairdressers. They take different courses. A few kids looked at me curiously as I came in. I sat down hastily, feeling like a wolf inadequately draped in sheepskin. Rufus Brown, the star of our basketball team, was in the seat ahead of me. He turned around in his seat and looked down at me. "You taking general science?" he said. "You sure you got the right room?"

I tried to manage a cheerful smile. "Uh, yes," I said. "I'm really interested in general science."

Rufus raised an eyebrow skeptically and turned away. So I want to understand our sewer system, I said to myself. Is that a crime?

The bell rang and Coach Griffin jogged into the classroom wearing a sweatshirt that had "Wolverton Wolverines" on it. He sat down on the desk and produced a roll book. "Class," he said, "I'm Coach Griffin and this is general science. Everybody in the right room?" A couple of faces turned toward me and I could feel myself growing red, but Coach Griffin didn't notice.

He started handing out some mimeographed sheets spelling out the awful things that would happen to people who didn't get their homework in. I had just taken out my pen to change the date that our community project was due, the way he told us to, when a skinny girl from the office came into the class and handed him a slip of paper. He looked at it, puzzled, as if he had just learned to read, and then said, "Corrie Lindgren to the office." He looked up. "Is Corrie Lindgren here?"

Everybody in the class was looking straight at me, so there wasn't any point in denying that I was there. I gathered up my books, stood up, and moved toward the door. All at once I remembered why I had always followed the rules. When you got caught breaking them it was so embarrassing.

I listlessly followed the monitor down the hall to the office. "You're supposed to see Miss Futch," she said, looking at me with ghoulish interest. "Maybe there's some bad news from home."

"I don't think so," I said.

She looked disappointed.

When we got to the main office, I walked back to Miss Futch's smaller cubicle and went in.

"Corrie," she said, "I'm sorry to say there's a little problem with your course schedule." Miss Futch is a rather large woman who wears her gray hair swept back into a fat bun. Her glasses are always slipping down her nose and she speaks with the speed of a glacier. I guess that's supposed to make her sound wise. She was holding a computer printout. She smiled at me. "This wonderful new computer of ours," she explained, "is making it possible for us to give each of our students more individual attention than was formerly possible."

I threw myself down on the cushy chair next to Miss

Futch's desk, resigned to the inevitable. She looked at me intently. "I wonder how you happened to sign up for general science, Corrie?"

"I like general science," I said doggedly. "I'm interested in general science."

"But general science is not a college-track course," she said. "And most important, it is not an elective. You know you must have an elective this year."

"It's not?" I said innocently. "I wasn't sure."

Miss Futch gave me a steely glance. "We must be well-rounded, Corrie. That is *most* important."

I didn't agree at all. Did anybody ever complain that Albert Einstein wasn't well-rounded? Did anybody ever say Margot Fonteyn should have taken home ec? It seemed to me that people should do what they like and are good at and not waste their time on other things, but I didn't say anything. I knew it was all over. I was going to have to take an elective.

Miss Futch picked up her pen. "How about home economics, Corrie? Every young girl needs to learn home economics."

Not young girls who plan to work and pay somebody else to make the beds, I thought. But it was the least distasteful of the alternatives, so I didn't protest. After all, according to Terri's big sister, the worst of it was listening to all of Mrs. Johnson's boring advice about womanhood. I thought I could put up with that.

Miss Futch acted as if she didn't trust me to go to the home economics class by myself; she actually walked me to the home ec building and handed me over personally to Mrs. Johnson. "A little change in scheduling," she murmured to Mrs. Johnson. "Corrie's going to be in your class this semester."

Terri waved at me from a table at the back of the classroom, and I went to sit near her. "Ooo la la!" she whispered to me. "Did you get caught?"

"Yup," I said.

"You'll never guess who's in our class!" she whispered.

I caught sight of Kel Reid looking back at me from the front of the class. Then Mrs. Johnson rapped a wooden spoon on the edge of her demonstration table for order. The class quieted down, and Kel turned his blue gaze toward Mrs. Johnson again, so all I could see was the back of his head. Kel Reid in home economics class? I looked at Terri and she nodded. She mouthed a word: "Unreal!"

"Now, uh, class," Mrs. Johnson said, "we have a lot of work to do this semester." She kept glancing uneasily at Kel. It was probably hard after so many years of saying "Now, girls" to have to switch gears. When the haze of shock had cleared from my eyes, I could see that Kel wasn't the only boy in the class either. Mason Miller, who I have known since my kindergarten days, was sitting right next to him.

Mrs. Johnson frowned. "Home economics is a serious discipline," she said. "An exacting course of study. There are many, many things we must cover, from the safe use of the microwave oven to the basics of tailoring, and that is only scratching the surface."

I was beginning to feel a little uneasy. So far Mrs. Johnson did not look like the friendly mother figure that Barbara had described to us. It was beginning to sound as if this course might mean work. And nobody knew better than I that if we got into serious work I was going to be in bad shape. I wondered whether it was too late for me to get into chorus. Singing dopey songs was beginning to look better and better to me. The only problem was that I knew that to switch at this point I would have to talk to Miss Futch again, and I wasn't sure I could take it.

As we all filed out of the classroom at the end of the period, I could see Mrs. Johnson looking rather desperately around her classroom kitchen as if wondering what in the world she was going to do to live up to the big introductory lecture. It hit me that maybe having boys in the class was having a strange effect on her, making her feel she had to measure up and show them how hard housework really was. Maybe Mrs. Johnson was one of those very old-fashioned types that was only moved into real action by the presence of a male to show off for. I saw Kel walking away from the building. If I have to spend a semester suffering through the higher levels of home economics, I thought bitterly, it's him I have to thank for it. I had no doubt that he was the one to blame. Good old Mason had never had an original thought in his life. I was sure it hadn't been his idea to sign up for home ec. Just the same, to check it out I trotted to catch up with Mason, who was walking ahead of me.

"Hi, Mason," I panted as I reached his side.

He looked at me with pleasure. I think Mason has always had a kind of crush on me. "Hi there, Corrie," he said. "Mrs. Johnson sure made home ec sound hard, didn't she?"

"She sure did. Whatever made you sign up for it in the first place?"

Mason's kind face looked a little puzzled. "I don't know," he said. "I guess it was Kel who gave me the idea. You know, he kind of pointed out to me how it was good to be independent and be able to do things for yourself. And, like, I love to eat and it would be good someday to be able to fix a decent meal and things like that."

"I see," I said. And I did. It was crystal clear. Kel, not being quite willing to be the only boy in the class, had fastened onto sweet old Mason and had shanghaied him into taking the course.

"Maybe it won't be as hard as it sounds," I said, trying hard to be optimistic.

"Gee, I hope not," said Mason. "You know, I haven't had much practice in cooking and sewing."

"Believe me, Mason," I said fervently, "you couldn't be in any worse shape than I."

It turned out the next week that the first thing we did in home ec was learn how to use a sewing machine. We each put a sheet of notebook paper into a machine and practiced stitching straight along the blue lines. I concentrated hard on that and thought I had done fine. But when we got our papers handed back the next day, mine was covered with red marks. It seemed you were supposed to stop when you got to the red ruled line. That had slipped my mind.

From then on things got harder fast. Terri reported that her sister Barbara said it hadn't been at all like that the year before. "Barb asked me if we had all sat around holding up pieces of different colored material next to our faces to decide what colors we looked best in. I told her we were too busy learning how to pin pleats, ease in, use tailor tacks, and cut on the bias,'' said Terri, sighing. She also told me that Barbara kept saying, ''Last year it was so easy. I don't understand it.'' But I understood it all right. Mrs. Johnson couldn't very well make Kel and Mason sit in front of a mirror holding up bolts of cloth to see what flattered their complexions, could she? So naturally she had to fill the class time that would have been spent doing something restful like that with time spent doing the harder stuff.

It was no time until we started right in making dresses, or ''an article of apparel,'' as Mrs. Johnson said, eyeing the boys nervously. The very thought of sewing a dress made me break out in a cold sweat. I had already flunked sewing on notebook paper. What was it going to be like when I met with real cloth?

As soon as Mrs. Johnson announced the date the sewing project would be due I went straightaway that afternoon to a fabric shop. Not only did I know I was going to need every minute I had to sew that thing, but I could see I should spend a lot of time choosing the pattern. I cannily reflected that careful groundwork here might save me from real disaster. What I needed was a dress with no collar, no sleeves, no darts, and preferably no seams. I thumbed through hundreds of sketches of chic designer fashions before I came up with a pattern humble enough for me. It closely resembled a potato sack and was labelled ''Very quick and easy.'' I took it to the checkout counter feeling smug.

A few days later in class, Mrs. Johnson beamed at us. ''Now, do we all have our patterns?'' she chirped. She was a dried-up looking little woman who wore support hose and sensible shoes. Normally she looked as if her feet hurt, but today she was excited. "I have a lovely surprise for you, gir—uh—class. As an extra added incentive for you all, we are going to have a fashion show during school assembly so you can model your sewing projects for everyone to admire," she said.

I saw Kel blanch, but he didn't take it any harder than I did. I don't think I'm vain, but I knew there was no way I was going to wear that potato sack in front of the entire student body.

"Do they let you exchange patterns?" I said softly to Terri.

So that was how I ended up working on a pattern that had a collar, long sleeves, and darts galore. Worst of all, it was lined. I suppose the top seamstress for a Paris fashion house could have whipped it up in a few days. For me it looked like the work of a lifetime.

Mrs. Johnson gave us time in class to work on our sewing projects, but I could see it wasn't going to be enough time for me. Every afternoon I carefully stuffed all my pattern pieces and pins and thread into a big paper sack to take with me and work on at home. Except for that my life went on as usual. I made the highest score in the class on the unit chemistry test, and Mr. March took me aside after class to ask whether I had ever considered a career in the sciences. Mrs. Elsmore read my essay on winter to the class and raved about my topic sentences and transitions. In home economics, Mason sneaked loving looks at me over his sewing machine and seemed to be working himself up to asking me out. But always hanging over me and taking the joy out of these little victories was

The Dress. You would have thought that dress was designed as punishment for my life of crime. Whenever I worked on it the pins got stuck in my fingers, and one time at home I actually leaned over too far, sewed my hair into a seam, and had to be rescued by Mom. It didn't get any better as I went on either. Whenever I was supposed to "ease in," I ended up with a funny-looking little pleat. And whenever I tried to clip a curve, if it didn't rip outright, it frayed. I tore out the seams in that dress and redid them so many times that the material started to look like gauze. Even Mom, who had always been so keen for me to learn a little home craft, felt sorry for me. She would come into the room where I sat at the sewing machine, lean over me, and murmur, "Oh, dear, Corrie. Oh, dear, dear."

In class, when I looked around I could see that lots of people were having trouble of one kind and another. Of course, nobody even came close to having the problems I was having. I was in a different category altogether. But Mason had trouble setting in the sleeves on his knit shirt, and Terri was going crazy pinning in the fifty little soft pleats on her dress. "They looked like gathers in the picture," she said bitterly. Even Peggy Slankard, who always said she wanted to be a dress designer, had second thoughts about the whole thing when her collar turned out lopsided.

One person who took to it as if he were born to be a seamstress though was Kel. Pins never attacked him. Scissors never took a nip out of his thumb. The cloth lay quietly while he worked it to his will. He was just naturally very neat with his hands. And he seemed actually to get a kick out of home ec. He kept making little cracks under his breath to Mason, and Mason would double over laughing. It would have been nice to be in on the jokes. It would have been nice even to feel cheerful enough in home ec to think about making a joke. All I did was sit there and suffer quietly.

Of course, unlike me, Kel hadn't tempted fate by picking a pattern with sleeves and a collar. He was making a hunting vest. When he brought in the pattern, Mrs. Johnson had looked at it doubtfully, but it was definitely a piece of wearing apparel, so he got by. The only thing that was the least bit tricky about it was sewing the hundreds of little pockets where shotgun shells were to fit in. That vest, fully loaded, would be capable of carrying pounds and pounds of ammunition. Sometimes when Kel and Mason were chortling way up front, I consoled myself by thinking about how I could just wait until Kel got the vest fully loaded, touch a match to it, and presto, he would go off like a rocket and land in the next county. Of course, there were no shells in it while he worked on it in class, but my guess was that he would come on the day of the fashion show with it fully stocked and with a shotgun as a stage prop. That way, he could walk across the stage covered with ammunition, carrying a gun, and nobody would dare to laugh at him for being in the fashion show.

Of course, I was devoting a lot of effort to making sure nobody laughed at me either. I worried about it a good bit. I was pretty sure that the mistakes I made with the seams wouldn't show. And all the matted mess of thread that somehow appeared whenever I sewed would be hidden underneath the material. But I had gotten to where I would wake up in the middle of the night feeling cold and thinking that maybe the skirt would manage to come unanchored and slowly slide to my ankles in front of the whole school. I concentrated all my work on making sure that wasn't going to happen and also on making sure the dress fit so that it would look all right on stage. The waist was a wreck, but I planned to cinch a wide belt around it to cover that up. I figured the belt would give extra security to the skirt too.

By spending every minute of my spare time for six weeks on the dress, I managed to finish it just in time for the fashion show. In spite of my best efforts using the hemming stitch, the hem had started to sag by the morning of the show. I patched it up as best I could with bits of tape. Mom put my hair up in a braided chignon that morning and let me drive her car so that I wouldn't have to take the dress on the crowded bus.

It was a cold and gloomy morning and it had started to rain, so we draped the dress in a plastic dry cleaner's bag to keep it dry. Mom helped me spread it out on the back seat so it wouldn't wrinkle. I appreciated her help, but I could have done without the way she kept clucking her tongue and saying, "Oh, dear, Corrie. Oh, dear."

I got into the front seat, pulled gloves onto my icy fingers, and said bravely, "It won't show from the stage, Mom."

"Of course not," said Mom. "And you certainly did your best."

I caught a glimpse of the dress in the back seat and shuddered a little. It was kind of awful to think that that was my best. It was lucky for me that I didn't live back in pioneer days when all you had to wear were the things you made yourself.

I turned on the ignition and pulled out of the driveway, trying to give Mom what I hoped was a confident and cheerful wave. The rain was the kind of cold, misty rain we get a lot of in February. All the cars had their headlights on, but they were just pale smudges in the foggy rain. It had been bitterly cold and nasty for days. I wished I were sitting by the fire instead of going out in the yuck to get to school. The only thing I could think of that was even remotely cheerful was that spring had to be coming soon.

When I got to school I lifted the hood of my raincoat carefully over my head so as not to disarrange the chignon, got the dress out of the back seat, and picked my way through the puddles to the auditorium. When I got backstage, most of the other members of the class were already dressed and standing there looking rather green with nervousness. I guess most of the kids had worn their outfits to school to save dressing backstage, but I hadn't wanted people to gather around me and tut-tut over my seams, so I was delaying getting into mine as long as possible. I wiped my damp shoes off with a tissue. Then I saw that Mason was sitting in a chair in the corner near the light switches looking miserable. I went over there carrying my dress in its plastic bag. "Hi, Mason," I said. "Where's Kel?"

"In the hospital," growled Mason. "I'll kill him for this. How could he do this to me?"

It didn't seem possible that I had heard him right. "You

said, in the hospital?'' I said. But I saw right away that Kel had hit on the only possible solution—the only way, really, he could get out of being in the fashion show. If he had just stayed home and said he had the sniffles, everyone would have said he had chickened out, but since he had actually managed to get himself put in the hospital, nobody could accuse him of that.

"How did he manage that?'' I asked with grudging admiration.

"Hunting accident,'' said Mason.

I steadied myself against the wall. "You mean he got . . . shot?'' I asked shakily.

"No,'' said Mason. "Fell into a beaver hole. Exposure. He's in for observation.''

Mason looked as if he would have been glad to share Kel's hospital bed.

Mrs. Johnson appeared at my side, glancing at her watch. "Corrie, you had better get dressed,'' she said. "We have only a few more minutes.''

I moved toward the dressing room as Mrs. Johnson started her pep talk. "Now, gir—uh—class,'' she said, "there's nothing to be nervous about. Just walk tall and gracefully or . . . uh . . . forcefully, as the case may be. Don't hurry. Just be calm.'' I closed the door of the dressing room, shutting off the sound of her voice, and stepped out of my skirt. What could a beaver hole be? I wondered. Did beavers dig underground like chipmunks? And how did you get exposure? I laid my regular clothes aside on a dusty chair and stepped into the dress. There was a rapping on the door of the dressing room. "Are you ready, Corrie?'' said Mrs. Johnson's voice. "We're about to begin.''

"Almost, Mrs. Johnson,'' I called. "I'll be there in a minute.''

I had worn my best slip just in case the dress fell apart somehow, but I was beginning to feel more confident. I was pretty sure it would hold together and look okay. And I wasn't worried about walking across the stage either. I told myself that if I could dance and swim, surely I could walk across the stage.

Just as I was coming out of the dressing room, Terri came dashing up the steps from the fire exit. "Car trouble,'' she panted. "I called you, but you'd already gone.''

"Shhh,'' said Mrs. Johnson, staring at us fiercely. The first girl was going on. I could hear the music, but I couldn't see what was happening on stage because too many kids had already clustered at the wings to peek out. A moment later, though, Stephanie reeled back into our midst and Mrs. Johnson shoved Beth out. Finally it was my turn. I walked out on stage feeling kind of short of breath and hot in the face. At first, seeing the sea of faces behind the footlights, I started to get dizzy. I had to look away quickly. The trick was not to look down, I decided. I managed to smile and concentrated on walking in time to the music. Listening to the music, I could almost pretend I was alone. I wheeled, turned, smiled again, and at last was off stage. I could hear applause. "You were great,'' whispered Mason.

One by one we each did a turn on stage and returned to

collapse in relief in the wing. When Terri came off she practically passed out in my arms. "I tripped," she said. "It was awful." It was worse, though, for Mason. His applause was mixed with some derisive hoots, and he came off stage red-faced.

"Well, it's over now, anyway," I said thankfully. I had made it. I had finished the dress on time and worn it in front of the whole student body without disaster. Now all I had to do was safety pin my name to it and hand it in to Mrs. Johnson for grading. She had put several large cardboard boxes by the door for us to drop the clothes into. Out in front of the stage I could hear the band playing the school song and then the sounds of hundreds of shuffling feet leaving the auditorium.

"Boy," said Terri, "I never thought I'd look forward to going to chemistry class."

"Mason says Kel is in the hospital," I said.

"What happened?" said Terri, her eyes widening. "Mason, have you seen him?"

While they talked, I went into the dressing room and changed into a more reliable outfit. I promised myself that I was never again going to complain about the cost of clothes. Now that I looked at my ordinary skirt and shirt with different eyes they looked like miracles of fine craftsmanship worth every penny I had spent. As for the dress I had made myself, I had already decided that when Mrs. Johnson got finished grading it, I was going to have a small private bonfire for it.

The next day Kel was back at school. I saw him outside in the center of a clump of boys. I guessed he was telling them about his hunting accident and the hospital, but you would have thought from the way he looked that he'd just got back from a party. Everybody around him was listening closely. I noticed that Mason hadn't stayed angry long. He was looking at Kel as wide-eyed as everybody else.

As I walked past I wondered what it would be like to have girls go red in the face when you spoke to them and to have boys falling all over you to hear every word you said. I couldn't see that there was anything so special about Kel.

A few days later, Mrs. Johnson handed back our sewing projects. It was another gray, rainy day with slivers of ice in the mud puddles. Only the crocuses under the tree next to the school entrance made you believe that spring was coming, and even the crocuses looked sad. Closed up tightly because of the gloom, they looked like short, fat carrots instead of flowers. To top off a perfectly awful day, Mrs. Johnson gave me an F on the dress.

I shouldn't have been surprised. I knew the dress was a disaster. But I had never gotten an F before in my whole life. It made me feel as if Mrs. Johnson were mad at me. And it was so unfair. Nobody could have worked harder on the thing than I had, nobody. Mom was right. I really had done my best. I hurried away from class, not wanting to talk to anybody for fear I would burst into tears. I hurried so fast I accidentally caught up with Kel. "Coming down with a cold?" he asked as I drew up to him. I didn't trust myself to say anything so I just walked faster and moved ahead of him. "Anything wrong?" he called. This was really the worst. Kel Reid was being nice to me. I must look pretty pitiful.

I dashed into the girls' room and threw cold water on my face. It was so cold that it shocked me out of feeling sorry for myself, but I longed to get home and have a good cry.

By the time I did get home that afternoon I felt sorrier than ever for myself. I went straight to my bedroom and cried. I really cried. I sobbed and pounded on my bed and kicked my feet and cried some more. Mom knocked quietly on my door. "Anything wrong, Corrie?" she asked. "May I come in?"

I just went on crying. She came in and sat on the bed. "What happened?" she asked.

"Mrs. Johnson failed me on the dumb dress," I sobbed.

Mom laughed. "Goodness, I'm glad that's all. I thought somebody had died."

I dabbed at my eyes with the corner of my pillowcase. "But it's so unfair," I wailed. "You know how hard I worked on that dress. She could at least have given me a D."

Mom stroked my hair. "I know, sweetheart. You did work hard, and I know it's disappointing, but you may as well face it—you're just going to have to be rich and famous because you'll never make it as a housewife."

In spite of myself, I giggled. I sat up, reached for a tissue, and blew my nose. "I don't want to make it as a housewife," I said, choking, "but I sure wouldn't mind being valedictorian. If I fail home ec it isn't going to help any. Wouldn't it be grim if old Otis Boggs got ahead of me because I failed home ec?"

"I can't believe failing home ec is going to ruin your

whole life," Mom said. "And being valedictorian isn't the be-all and end-all of existence, you know." But a minute later she said, "Is the sewing project really such a big part of your grade?"

"Absolutely an enormous part," I wailed. "The only thing that counts as much is the free project due at the end of the term, and Mrs. Johnson is pushing everybody to do more sewing for that!"

"But you don't have to do sewing?"

"No, but if you don't you've got to think up something else to do."

"I think you'd better think up something else, then, don't you?"

"Golly, yes." I groaned. "But what?"

I was already starting to feel better, though. I could see that I had made a serious tactical error in not sticking with the potato-sack pattern. Even if everybody had positively roared at it, the humiliation would have been over in a minute and I might at least have scraped a C or a D out of Mrs. Johnson. But that was over and done with. Now I had to figure out a way to climb out of this hole. If only I could make an A on my special project I could pull this grade up. Wasn't there anything in the field of home economics that I was any good at? Anything at all?

3

The next week made it even more clear that I was going to have to come up with a super-special project: on Friday I failed bed making. I never had a prayer. First, I completely forgot to fluff up the pillows. Then I just didn't have the knack of making hospital corners with the sheets, and when my corners popped out I was so demoralized I didn't try to make sure the sides of the sheets were even. Also, I didn't check when I was finished to make sure the stripes on the bedspread were straight. I could see Mrs. Johnson shaking her head as she marked down a grade for my performance in her roll book. My situation was desperate.

All the other kids in the class, the kids who could sew and make beds, were leaning back and relaxing without a thought for tomorrow, but I couldn't afford to do that. I had to come up with an idea to save my skin. In my mind, one by one I went over all the household skills I could think of and asked myself whether there was any hope that I could impress Mrs. Johnson with the way I did any of them. Cooking? Could I present my vegetable noodle soup, which I make by mixing a can of vegetable soup with a can of noodle soup? I was afraid I was going to have to come up with something more impressive than that—a five-course dinner of French cooking, at least. And I knew better than to try such a thing. I had learned my lesson with the dress. This time I had to be careful to choose something that I knew I could do a good job on. But what? Child care? Difficult to lay hands on a kid for that one.

I thought and thought. In fact, I was thinking so hard one day right after school that I ran smack into Kel in the hall. It was embarrassing. There I was with all my books bouncing around me while he stood with a firm grip on his. I bent down to pick mine up, blushing. Unluckily, he bent down at the same time to help me and we bumped again.

"Excuse me," I muttered, gathering up my books.

"Are you all right?" he asked.

"Fine," I said. I scooted away down the hall as fast as I could. It wasn't just Kel's superior look that got on my nerves or his everlasting hunting. It was that I knew he was the one responsible for my horrible troubles in home ec. If only he hadn't decided to take home ec, it would still be the peaceful, boring course Barbara had breezed through, instead of this souped-up, roast-you-over-hot-coals version that was killing me.

I was glad to get out of the musty halls of the school.

Outside it was sunny, with a fresh, damp earth smell in the air. It seemed as if it was the first day in weeks that it hadn't been raining, sleeting, or slinging frozen rain about. Everybody was milling around waiting for school buses or else walking toward the parking lot, whooping and calling to each other almost in a carnival atmosphere. The crocuses outside the entrance were wide open in the sunshine, their shiny petals glistening. They looked much prettier that way than closed up, looking like carrots. Suddenly the answer to my problem hit me like a burst of light. Carrots! That was the answer. I had it! I would grow a vegetable garden.

The more I turned it over in my mind, walking in the direction of my bus, the more I knew I had a winner. I loved plants. And I had a green thumb. Hadn't I sprouted an avocado seed? Hadn't I grown a sweet potato vine on the kitchen windowsill? Of course, so far my green thumb hadn't had much scope because of Dad being so devoted to our lawn. He had spent practically his whole life getting it to look velvety like a golf green, and he had never allowed anybody to plow up his precious turf just to plant flowers or vegetables. I was sure, though, that when I explained to him how desperate my situation was, he would come around. After all, this was no little whim. I *needed* to grow a vegetable garden.

Already the project was taking shape in my mind. I would get books from the library that explain how to grow a vegetable garden. I planned to make a record of the progress of the garden step by step with Dad's camera. When we turned in our projects in May, I was sure Mrs. Johnson would be awed by my research, my hard work, and above all, by my basket brimming with the luscious produce of my garden. Corrie, I said to myself, this time you've got it! A stroke of pure inspiration.

That night at dinner we had roast beef and lemon meringue pie, Dad's favorites. I knew that while he was in a mellow mood because of the roast beef, it was a good time to mention my project.

"I don't suppose it's a secret," I said as I passed Dad the green beans, "that I need to bring up my grade in home ec."

"I'm not surprised," said Tim, snickering.

"Hush, Tim," said Mom.

I ignored him. "Luckily, I have come up with a great idea for my final project," I said. "This could make a big difference to me. It's really important."

I glanced at Dad to see how he was taking the buildup, but so far he didn't look too impressed.

"The thing is," I said, coming out with it suddenly, "I have to grow a vegetable garden."

Dad calmly ladled some gravy onto his plate. "That sounds like a good idea, Corrie, but just where do you imagine you could put such a garden?"

"I sort of thought in the backyard where the sun is good."

"You mean right in the middle of the backyard?" Dad said, wincing as if I had proposed cutting out a pound of his own flesh. "I can't have you doing that. Why, it might take a decade for the lawn to recover! You know how I've slaved on that lawn. Ever since you were a baby. Battling the insects. Balancing the nutrients. Rolling it. Using an electric lawn mower so as not to butcher the blades of grass." His voice took on a tender sound. There was no doubt about it, when you get Dad started on the lawn he could sound like a first-class nut. This was beginning to look harder than I had thought.

Mom brought out the pie and Dad beamed at it, poising his fork in readiness.

"Dad . . ." I began.

"Please, Corrie," he said, "let's discuss this after dinner, if you don't mind."

Mom smiled. I was glad she could see a little humor in it. I had always thought that the way Dad babied the lawn was kind of funny myself, but tonight it was taking on a sinister look. I mean, what was more important, the lawn or his own daughter? Was he going to end up feeding his family to the compost heap next?

When we had finished with the pie I helped Mom clear the table.

"Mom!" I said in a low voice. "What am I going to do? This is serious."

"Don't worry about it, sweetheart. Have you ever known your father to be unreasonable?"

I thought he had done a pretty good imitation of it at dinner, actually, but I didn't like to say so.

"He'll come around," Mom said. "It's just going to take him a while to get used to the idea."

After Mom and I loaded the dishes in the dishwasher, the doorbell rang. It was Miss Addie, who lives in the house directly behind us. She was a very interesting old lady who had spent her whole life doing adventurous things. She had been an aviator in Africa, for example. At one time she had worked in the Peace Corps in Afghanistan. But finally she realized she was getting old, so she came back here to Wolverton to retire and moved in with her stay-at-home sister Bertha, who had lived in the house behind us forever. The strange thing was that Miss Addie, who had been in plane wrecks and had had typhoid and dysentery, was still going strong, but she hadn't been home a month before Bertha had a heart attack and died. It was very sad. Dad said that Addie blamed herself for not coming back sooner so that she and Bertha could have enjoyed some of their old age together.

Miss Addie didn't look at all like most of the old ladies I knew in Wolverton, pink and fluffy and round. She had yellowish, wrinkled skin and short white hair, wore slacks, and looked as tough as shoe leather. I took her coat from her and hung it up.

"Evenin', Corrie. Evenin', George, Margaret. I haven't come by for a long visit. Just came to tell you I'm going down to Florida for a while."

"Do have a cup of coffee, Addie," Mom said.

"Well, maybe one cup," said Miss Addie, settling into Dad's armchair and crossing her legs. She was wearing blue sneakers with beige pants.

"We'll be sorry to see you go," said Dad, "but I can understand your getting fed up with this weather."

"It's not that," said Miss Addie. "I've never minded a little cold and rain. No—it's sitting around that house of Bertha's. It gets me down. It's not really my place, you know. Every bit of the stuff in it was Bertha's, and it reminds me of her so much I get to feeling right low. I'm going to go south, visit friends, and decide what I want to do with the place. Maybe I'll decide to come back when I'm feeling a little more cheerful, but I can't be sure.''

"We'll be happy to keep an eye on it for you," said Dad.

"That's kind of you, George. But young Marshall Felton has said he'd like to do that. I'm going to pay him a little bit to go in and check the thermostat, run the water now and then, and generally keep watch on things while I'm gone.''

I was surprised that Marshall had volunteered to house sit. I wouldn't have thought he'd be interested in doing something for "a little money." At the rate he spent money on skiing, clothes, and his car you wouldn't have thought he would even notice a *little* money.

Miss Addie turned her bright eyes toward me. "Tell me what you're doing in school these days, young lady.''

"I'm trying to bring up my home economics grade," I said grimly. "I think I can do it if Dad will just let me use part of the backyard for a vegetable garden.''

Dad gave me a look. "Corrie, we'll talk about that later.''

Mom showed up with a tray and served coffee; Miss Addie leaned forward to put six sugars in hers. "It would be a shame to plow up that beautiful grass of yours, George," she said.

"That's what I've been saying," muttered Dad.

"Why don't you let Corrie do her garden in my backyard?" she said, stirring her coffee, which was as thick as syrup.

"I couldn't let her do that," said Dad, startled.

"Don't see why not. Bertha's grass was nothing to boast about, poor soul. And I've got more yard back there than anybody could ever possibly use."

Miss Addie's house was actually built on two lots. Her house was directly behind ours, but her yard extended all the way back behind the Reids' house.

"It would be too much of an imposition," said Dad, but I could see he was warming to the idea. It would be the perfect solution to his problem. It would be perfect for me too. I knew I could have a bigger garden on Miss Addie's land than Dad would ever let me have in our backyard.

"That's awfully nice of you," I chimed in.

"Are you sure it won't be an imposition?" Mom said.

"Oh, no," said Miss Addie. "I don't care anything about the yard." She rose creakily. "Thanks for the coffee. I've got to go finish my packing now."

I ran to fetch her coat. This was a piece of luck I hadn't counted on. In Miss Addie's yard I could have a perfectly fantastic garden with no protests from Dad.

The next day after school I went to the library and checked out some gardening books. I also sent off for some seed catalogues. The seed catalogues arrived in no time, and they made much better reading than the gardening books. The gardening books were full of discouraging sections on bugs and diseases. And it didn't sound very likely that I could meet their high standards for soil preparation. According to them I was going to need wheelbarrowloads of manure, peat moss, sand, and compost. And all that was supposed to be dug in and beaten up like scrambled eggs into a fine, "friable" mass, whatever that meant. I wasn't at all sure I could manage it. It sounded like more the sort of thing for a person who had a tractor or four or five gardeners, at least. For me, even digging up the grass to make a place for the garden was going to be a big problem.

The seed catalogues were much more cheerful than the gardening books. To read them you'd think all you had to do was drop the seed in the ground and stand back. The pictures showed great big, perfect heads of broccoli and cabbage, beautiful, svelte green beans, and enormous watermelons. The world as pictured in seed catalogues was sunny and bright. There wasn't even any mention of dirt.

"Look at this, Dad," I said one evening as I was sitting cosily by the fire contentedly poring over a seed catalogue. "Here's a new variety of thick-walled, fast-growing green pepper!"

Dad peered over my shoulder at the lush illustration and said dampeningly, "There's many a slip 'twixt the cup and the lip."

That's not the kind of upbeat encouragement a beginning gardener needs. I decided Dad's long battle with the bugs and the weeds in the grass had left him disillusioned. I didn't let him discourage me. I sat down with a sheet of graph paper and carefully planned every inch of my garden, just the way they tell you to do it in the gardening books. I was prepared to go to any lengths, to brave any difficulties, in order to have a fantastic garden that would bring my grade up. I was anxious to start work. All I needed was for spring to come. Meanwhile I sent off for my seeds.

When Terri came over a couple of weeks later, she was

very impressed by my efforts. She looked at my graph with great respect. "Neat, Corrie," she said. "When do you actually get to plant the seeds?"

"I've already planted some," I said proudly. I led her back to my room where a large fluorescent plant light stand with black iron legs glowed with its eerie blue-white light over my little plastic flower pots. It looked like some extra-terrestrial spider set on devouring a broccoli sprout.

"Gee," she said. "Are those your plants and stuff?"

"Yup," I said. "Some of them. I have to get a head start, you see. When it gets a little warmer I'll put them out in the garden with hot caps."

"What are hot caps?" she asked.

"Little waxed-paper tents for each plant, to protect them from the cold."

"I didn't realize there was so much to this garden stuff," she said.

"I'm taking pictures of every step," I said. "I want Mrs. Johnson to see just how much work goes into this sort of thing. Come on into the kitchen and see my germination center."

I scrambled up the kitchen stool and took down a couple of the six-pack sets of little plastic flower pots in which I had started my seeds. They were all covered up with old plastic bread wrappings to keep the moisture in. "They like it up here where it's warm," I explained, handing one down to Terri. "Another good place is on top of the water heater. I'm thinking of trying the furnace room next. I'm running out of space here."

Terri looked at the little plastic flat. "But this is just dirt," she said.

"It's potting soil with vermiculite mixed in," I corrected her. "The seeds are in there, but you just can't see them yet. I check them every day, and the minute they sprout I move them into my room under the light."

Terri looked as if she had found out all she wanted to know about the care and feeding of seedlings, but she tried to be polite. "When do they actually go into the garden?" she said. "I mean, spring is pretty much here, isn't it? The daffodils are blooming and everything."

"Well, I haven't actually dug the garden out yet," I admitted. "It's going to be a terrible job, and it isn't exactly warm yet."

"Aren't you going to have to do it pretty soon, though?" she asked.

I cast a glance outside the kitchen windows to the back fence, where the cold wind was tossing the daffodils. "Yes," I said reluctantly, "I need to get out there and get to work." The thought of it made me shiver. It came on me forcibly that I was really a cat kind of person. I liked warm patches of sunlight. I liked to sit by the fire. I preferred to look at early spring flowers by peeking out a window. To get a garden started the proper time of year, you needed a dog type of person, a person who didn't mind discomfort and nasty weather, who enjoyed grubbing around in the mud—a person like Kel Reid, for example. Of course, there was no chance I was going to turn into someone like that, but it would have been nice at least, I thought wistfully, to have battery-heated socks. "I'm going to get down to it any day now," I said. "Want some cocoa?"

Mom and Tim had gone on a Boy Scout trip, so the house was blissfully quiet. It was a perfect time for Terri to pour out her heart to me, and she didn't waste any time beginning once we sat down with the cocoa. "Joe is a special kind of person," she said, "and I'm very fond of him. But Eric is so *interesting*."

"You're going to regret this, Terri," I said.

"I'll only be young once," she said, paying no attention. "Do I want to waste all my time being sensible?"

"I don't know . . . it seems like a good idea to me," I said.

"I don't," she said positively. "I want excitement. I want adventure. In other words—I want Eric."

Eric Tullis was an enormous senior who was at his best grinding his cleats into his opponents faces on the football field. It had never crossed my mind that he might have a more tender side.

"Is Eric acting interested in you?" I said.

She blushed. "Well," she said, "yesterday he said he thought he'd dropped his contact lens down my dress."

Really, it was hopeless. If this was Terri's idea of a winning come-on, she was past good advice.

"I don't know him very well yet," Terri admitted, "but I think he's more the strong, silent type."

Like King Kong, I thought.

"I think underneath he's quite sensitive," she said.

"What makes you think that?" I asked.

"I just know," she said. "You can tell about these things. I think he's actually a kind, sensitive person with this rough macho shell."

Terri and I had been friends so long I felt I had to point out a slight flaw in her reasoning. "Don't you think," I suggested tentatively, "that it might be better not to brush off Joe, who you know for *sure* is a kind, sensitive person?"

"You haven't been listening to me, Corrie," said Terri reproachfully. "I told you I wanted adventure."

I began to understand those country-and-western songs that moan about somebody standing by to pick up the pieces. I didn't exactly expect that Eric was going to grind his cleats into Terri's face, but I had the strong feeling that nothing good was going to come of this.

"Just what do you mean by adventure?" I inquired delicately.

"Adventure is getting to know someone entirely different from you," said Terri. "Like it would probably do you good to get to know Kel . . . it would broaden your horizons."

"No, thanks," I said. "I'll let you have the adventure for both of us. I hope getting to know Eric will be very rewarding for you." I couldn't quite stifle a smile at the thought, though. Terri shot me a black look. "I'm sorry I let out a teensie little smile about Eric," I said guiltily, "but the idea takes some getting used to."

"Of course, he hasn't asked me out yet," said Terri, somewhat mollified.

"He will, though," I said. I thought of all kinds of good advice to give Terri as she started out on her big romantic adventure with King Kong—things like, remember never to go out with someone who can't spell his own name, never date a boy whose expression frightens your dog, and avoid dating boys who eat their hamburger raw. But I could tell she didn't have any sense of humor about Eric, and after I had slipped up with that fatal little smile, I decided I had better not say anything. I figured all the practice using self-control would come in handy later when I had to stop myself from saying "I told you so."

4

Of course, I knew Terri was right about the garden. I had to get out there and work on it whether I wanted to or not, so the next day after school I put on some woolen pants, woolen socks, and my old loafers. Then I pulled a sweater on over my shirt and added a sweat shirt and an old corduroy blazer for good measure. I peeked out the window at the wind tossing the daffodils about and decided to wrap a wool scarf around my head. Fully protected against the cold, I was just starting toward the back door when Tim yelled, "Look at Corrie, Mom. She looks like an Eskimo." He chortled. "Are you warm enough, Corrie?"

Mom peeked out the kitchen door and said, "Get some gloves, Corrie, or you'll end up with blisters when you dig."

"Jeez," said Tim. "What about an overcoat? What

about knee boots? Don't forget your ear muffs! You'd think she was headed for the North Pole, for Pete's sake."

I ignored him and went back to get some gloves from my dresser drawer. The problem with this outfit, I thought as I returned with the gloves, was that what with all the layers of shirt, sweater, sweat shirt, and blazer, it was hard for me to bend my arms. I didn't have much experience with digging, but I thought I would probably have to bend my arms.

I went outside and headed for the utility shed to get a shovel, the wind whistling around my ears. A cheerful thought struck me. Maybe the soil would be too wet and clumpy to work. The gardening books had stated very clearly that it wasn't smart to work the soil when it was too wet. Unfortunately, it had been a few weeks since our last dreary rain and I was afraid I couldn't count on the soil being too soggy to work with. I got a big shovel out of Dad's storage shed, unlatched the back gate, and went on into Miss Addie's yard. She had certainly been right when she said the grass was nothing to brag about. There were clumps of yellow crabgrass all over the place and tufts of dandelions and other weeds among the grass. Dad would have croaked if his lawn looked like that. I went to the back of the lot, behind the Reids' house, where the sun was brightest. The wind stung my cheeks, so I wrapped the woolen scarf more closely around my face and gritted my teeth. I tried to stick the shovel into the ground. It wouldn't go in. I tried again, this time pushing it with my foot. Still no luck. I peered at the ground, wondering if there was a rock or something there, but there wasn't. Just grass—thick, tightly growing matted yellow grass. It might not look beautiful, but it sure had a firm grip on the dirt.

"How's it going?" Kel called to me.

I jumped. I saw then that he was leaning over his own back fence watching me at work. He was wearing some sort of blue checked wool jacket open at the neck and the wind was blowing his hair in front, but in spite of not being very wrapped up, he looked warm. As I felt my fingers turn to ice, it was easy for me to dislike him.

"I can't seem to get the shovel to go in," I admitted. "The grass is so thick."

"Maybe you need to sharpen your shovel," he said.

"Sharpen my shovel?" It sounded like a weird thing to do to a shovel.

"Here, let me give it a try," he said. Putting one hand on the fence, he vaulted over it.

I handed him the shovel. "I'm trying to get a garden started back here," I explained, "for my home ec project."

He immediately plunged the shovel down to the hilt through the thick mat of grass into the dirt. I looked at him in amazement. "How did you do that?" I said.

"It's not hard," he said. "Want me to cut up the sod for you? Just to get you started?"

Actually, what I wanted was not to owe him any favors, but I reminded myself that this was no time to stand on pride. My survival was at stake here. Did I want to pass home ec or not? And after all, it was his fault that I was failing home ec in the first place. Why shouldn't he help me out?

I swallowed hard. "That would be very nice," I said faintly.

Kel looked amused. Now that I saw him in the bright spring sunlight I noticed for the first time that his face had that faint warm, toasted look that in blonds passes for a suntan. I guessed he was outside so much he kept a tan all year round.

"Just mark out where you want the garden to be," he said. "Then I'll cut the sod out." He picked up a stick and tossed it to me. "You can mark the corners with this," he said.

I fumbled the stick and dropped it. I saw that he was grinning. Really, he was infuriating. Not everybody could be good at catching things, after all. I stooped to pick it up. I knew the dimensions the garden was going to have to be because even though I hadn't brought my graph outside I had worked on it so long that I had memorized it, so I stuck the stick into the ground, confidently paced off the distance to the next corner, and marked that with another stick.

Kel whistled. "That big?" he said. "Why does it have to be so big?"

"To impress Mrs. Johnson," I said. "I need something really great to impress her with after the disaster I had with the sewing project."

He threw a shovelful of sod easily aside. "Too bad I had to miss that home ec fashion show," he said, not looking a bit sorry. "I didn't get to see anybody's sewing projects after they were finished."

"Whatever happened to you that day, anyway," I

asked, stamping my feet to keep warm. "Mason was pretty mad that you didn't make it. How did you manage to end up in the hospital?"

He leaned on the shovel for a minute. I could see he was going to enjoy telling me about it. "You see," he said, "I was out duck hunting and got separated from the others, so I was quietly wading with hip boots through a creek on my way back to the truck. Then suddenly, wham! I was down in the water up to my chin. I had stepped into a beaver hole. Lucky thing I didn't break a leg. I hung onto my gun and fought against the current. It was freezing in there. In fact, I think the only thing that saved my life was that Mom had just fed us a big breakfast with pancakes and sorghum syrup. If it had been plain blood in my veins I would have frozen stiff and been a goner, but luckily I had all this sorghum syrup in me acting like antifreeze. So then I clawed my way up the bank with my fingernails and staggered in the direction of the truck more dead than alive. What happened then is that when I got in the truck I passed out on the horn. When Dad and the others heard the horn blaring, they all came running and drove me to the hospital."

I looked at him incredulously. "And you call hunting *fun?*" I said.

"Everybody's got to have a hobby," he said gravely. He went back to his digging.

"You could have been killed."

He shrugged. I guess he figured he hadn't been killed, so what was the fuss about?

"I can't understand why you want to shoot poor

harmless ducks, anyway," I burst out. I hadn't really intended to say that, but it just came out.

He stopped digging a minute and looked at me in surprise. "It's no different from killing chickens and steers. You eat them, don't you?"

I didn't like to think about chickens and steers, and as long as they came cut up and in plastic-wrapped packages, I didn't have to. "I think it would be better to be a vegetarian," I said firmly.

I guess he could tell the whole thing really bothered me, because he didn't make some crack. He just kept shoveling. The garden was starting to take shape now. He was a very efficient digger. After a while he stopped and took off his jacket. Then he shoveled some more. There was no denying that all that shoveling was an awful lot of work. I could see I was building up a pretty sizable obligation here. I noticed something interesting as he worked, though. That cold, piercing glance that so unraveled my nerves was obviously just Kel's way of looking at things. He looked at clumps of dirt the same way, and I could hardly think he was trying to intimidate them. He just had this very attentive, steady way of looking at things that took a little getting used to. Finally, after endless shoveling, he finished.

"I think that's it," he said, wiping his brow with the sleeve of his shirt.

"It was awfully nice of you to do it for me," I said. I stood there awkwardly for a minute and finally said, "Would you like to come in the house and have some cocoa?"

"Okay," he said.

When we got to the back door, he had to take off his boots because the soles had great globs of damp clay stuck to them. I couldn't help noticing the boots. They looked clumsy enough to fit Donald Duck and were sort of grungy looking. "Are those your hunting boots?" I asked, trying not to sound repelled.

He looked at them affectionately. "Yup, those are the best you can buy."

I looked at them dubiously. They weren't at all like the shiny black boots I had seen in prints of men in red coats chasing foxes. They were more a grungy brown color and had about as much shine as if they'd been polished with peanut butter. "Do hunting boots always look like that?" I said.

"They do if you've enjoyed them for a long time," he said, smiling at me.

Then, while I stood there on the back stoop with the wind shriveling my lips, he carefully pointed out their many good features. It seemed they had a double layer of leather for protection against cold and damp, and there was something extra special about the shoelaces that allowed you to pull them tight with one tug. This was desirable for some reason. There was no use my trying to understand this hunting business. It was another world. The funny thing, I thought, was that Kel did not appear to be bloodthirsty, judging by his looks and actions.

I pushed open the back door and he followed behind me. I immediately started peeling off my blazer, sweat shirt, and sweater and piled them on a chair. Mom looked up from her mending. "Mom, this is Kel Reid from next door," I said. "He's been helping me dig the garden." I felt a little guilty saying that he'd been helping me, since so far I hadn't done anything at all, so I went on quickly. "I thought I'd fix us some cocoa."

I went into the kitchen and got down the packets of cocoa powder and the mugs. We always keep hot water on in the coffee pot, so all I had to do was pour the water in and stir vigorously, as the package tells you to. I was very proud of the way I could make lump-free instant cocoa. It needed a certain flick of the wrist to get those lumps out, but I had mastered it. When I came into the living room with the tray, Mom and Kel were talking, Kel wiggling his toes in his stocking feet. When he took his first sip of cocoa his face registered mild shock.

"I hope you like instant cocoa," Mom said.

"I don't think I've ever had it before," he said, looking at it distrustfully.

To me this showed that his poor mother was a slave to the stove, keeping five boys fed with everything made from scratch.

Mom snipped a thread. "Corrie tells me you're taking home economics," she said. "What made you decide to take that?"

Kel's suntan slowly took on a deeper flush. I had never seen him look uncomfortable before, and it was very interesting to watch. "You know how it is when you're one of five boys," he said. "It's like living in a locker room. Thought I'd see how the other half lives, that sort of thing."

Mom tucked her sewing back into her basket. "Seems like a good idea. Everyone should know how to do things around the house. Well, I'd better get down to the washing. If you kids need anything, just let me know."

She had no sooner disappeared in the direction of the laundry room than Kel said, "So your mom thinks everybody should be able to do things around the house? You must be a big disappointment to her."

I could feel tears starting to sting my eyes. I thought that was such a low, nasty thing to say I couldn't speak.

"I was just teasing," he said contritely. "Who cares whether you can sew or not? It's no big deal."

"I can do things that I like to do, just as you can do things that you like to do," I said.

He tactfully turned away to look at the photos on the piano so I could have the chance to dab at my eyes and blow my nose. "Is this one you?" he said, looking at a black-and-white shot of me.

"Yes," I said, sniffling. It was a picture of me hanging onto the edge of the pool with my hair all wet, and it wasn't exactly a glamour shot, but it was taken by Henry Adamson, the famous photographer, whom we had met one summer on vacation. He had signed it himself: *To Corrie, who swims like a fish and dances like an angel.* "You see, there are some things I can do," I said.

He looked around at me in surprise. "I never said there weren't," he said.

"You just make me feel like such a klutz," I said.

"I'm sorry," he said.

Now I had really done it, I thought. Now I looked like

not just a klutz but an insecure, awkward, crazy klutz. Why did I have to go and blurt out all those things? I sighed deeply. "Want some more cocoa?" I said. Then I noticed that his first cup was almost untouched and said, "Or some cookies?"

"I'd better be getting home," he said.

I walked him to the back door and watched him deftly tighten up the laces on his boots with a single tug. "Thanks again for the help," I said.

"Sure, any time," he said.

He walked away with those long, easy strides of his, leaving me wishing that I felt calm and superior the way he did. But as I closed the door and headed back toward my room, I realized I was being too hard on myself. After all, most of the time I got along fine. It was just that the combination of Kel Reid and home economics was turning me into a nervous wreck, that's all. I was going to have to get a grip on myself. What I felt I should do was get down to my chemistry homework. That was something I knew I could do without dissolving into tears. Before I could turn to go up to my room, though, Terri burst in the front door.

"Don't tell me," she said breathlessly. "Was that Kel Reid I just saw walking away from this house?"

"That was him," I said.

She threw herself on the sofa. "Tell me what he's really like," she said.

"I thought you were after Eric Tullis," I said.

"I am. In fact, I just came over to give you the latest installment. Guess what? He's asked me out!"

"That's nice," I said.

"There's just this one problem," she said, looking at me guiltily. "I'm afraid to go."

"So don't go," I said. It was hard for me to keep my mind on Terri's problems just then.

"I told him I didn't think my mother would let me go out alone with a senior," she said, looking guiltier than ever. "I just said that. Actually, the truth is that sometimes when I look at him it gives me chills. The wrong kind of chills."

"It's the fangs," I said. "You'll get used to it. Who are you getting to double with you?"

"You," she said.

"Me?" I screeched. "Me?"

"Well, you are my best friend. I'd do it for you, you know that."

"Be reasonable, Terri," I said. "It's not as if I'm going with somebody. Do you expect me just to tag along by myself to make sure Eric doesn't turn into a werewolf at the full moon or something?"

"Eric can fix you up with somebody," she said quickly.

I imagined a gallery of Eric's friends, with their twenty-inch biceps and their look of being fugitives from a pro football team. "No," I said.

"What about Marshall?" Terri said. "Eric could fix you up with Marshall. You know him. Oh, Corrie, I'd do it for you."

I could feel my voice growing a little bit strained. "Look, Terri," I said, "I understand why you don't want to be alone with Eric. I mean, he looks like something out of a prehistoric cave. Who can be sure he's even a hundred percent homo sapiens? But what I don't understand is why you don't just say no."

"I want to say I've been out with Eric one time," Terri said pleadingly. "I just want to have the chance to date one of those big, humungous football guys. You know, it'll be an experience."

I began to see what was going on. Terri was in the grip of that sort of insane emotion that makes people go over Niagara Falls in a barrel, storm the peaks of Mount Everest, and break the pie-eating record of the *Guiness Book of World Records*. I understood what was going on with *her,* all right. What I never did figure out, though, was what made me finally agree to go along with the scheme and say that I would go out with Marshall one more time to help her out. I had a hard time explaining it to myself. I had an even harder time explaining it to Mom later.

"But I thought you didn't like Marshall, Corrie," she said.

"He's not so bad," I said.

"I distinctly remember you saying you were never going to go out with him again," she said.

"It's a favor for Terri," I said.

"I don't think it's very kind to Marshall," said Mom severely. "He's going to get the idea that you like him."

"Oh, I don't think so," I said.

"I don't think it was very smart, either," Mom said. "You know, in a town like this if you go out with somebody twice, the next thing you know people are saying you're going steady."

"It's too late now, Mom." I sighed. "I've already told Terri I would do it." I realized it was the old marshmallow heart that had tripped me up again.

The next day I had the nursery deliver three bales of peat moss and once again took my shovel into Miss Addie's yard. We had had a sudden turn of the weather the way you do in March, and suddenly it felt like spring outside. The sun was shining everywhere; the air was still and almost warm. It was a perfect day to dig peat into the garden, and a single glance told me that this was a garden that really needed it. The plot Kel had hacked out for me was big and nicely squared off, but the dirt looked raw and red. In some places the clay was so pure it looked like slick white modeling clay. It was going to take a lot of peat and manure to make this stuff into something little broccoli plants would enjoy. I rolled one of the giant plastic-encased bales of peat over onto the plot and slit it open with a knife.

"Hi, there," said Kel.

I looked up and there he was, leaning on his fence. "Hi," I said.

"Mind if I watch?" he said.

"Uh, no, of course not," I said. After somebody has done an hour of shoveling for you, you aren't in any position to tell them to buzz off. Besides, I was glad to see him. It was nice to have somebody to talk to. I upturned a shovelful of clay and mixed the black peat in. It certainly didn't look friable yet. It just looked like clumps of clay with clumps of peat in it. But after all, I was only beginning.

"I'm sorry I made that crack about your sewing," he said.

"That's all right," I said.

"I didn't mean to hurt your feelings."

"I'll live," I said, plugging away at the shoveling. "I know I don't really have any business being in home ec. Heaven knows I tried to get out of taking an elective altogether, but I got caught. Then Miss Futch suggested home ec and I said okay, because from everything I'd heard it was easy. Terri's sister said that until this year mostly all Mrs. Johnson had done was stand around and give advice about being a woman." I leaned on my shovel and looked at him accusingly.

"You mean . . ."

"That's right," I said. "You and Mason have ruined a perfectly good snap course just by being there. Obviously she couldn't stand around giving advice about womanhood to you two."

If I had thought Kel would be sorry for what he had done, I was disappointed. He nearly choked laughing. "Watch out," I said coolly, "or you're going to pitch right over the fence." I went back to my shoveling. As soon as Kel stopped laughing, he offered to bring a shovel out and help me. "It's the least you can do," I said.

"I'm sorry to miss out on all Mrs. Johnson's advice about being a woman," he said, as he brought his shovel into the garden. "I'll bet it was a stitch."

With Kel helping out, the work went a lot faster. It wasn't just that it was good to have an extra shovel at work. It was also that it was a lot less boring when somebody else was around to talk to. "Well, at least *you* don't have anything to worry about in that class," I said. "You're good at home ec."

"I'll make some woman a wonderful husband, all right," he said, throwing a shovelful of dirt up in the air exuberantly so that it showered down in all directions.

"Why did you act embarrassed when Mom asked you about it?" I asked curiously.

"I guess I felt a little funny about it," he said. "It's just that your mother doesn't know me, and I was afraid she'd think I was weird or something. You don't want the very first thing that people find out about you to be that you take home ec. It seemed like a fun thing to do when I got Mason to sign up for it with me, you know—something different. But I have to say it's gotten sticky sometimes."

"Like the fashion show," I said.

"I'll say," he agreed heartily. "Until I lucked out and ended up in the hospital I was thinking there was only one way I was going to go across that stage and that was feet first. How could she do that to Mason and me? I couldn't believe it!"

It *was* pretty insensitive of Mrs. Johnson when I thought about it. No imagination, that was her problem. She probably just couldn't picture how Kel and Mason would feel. Kel efficiently turned over spadeful after spadeful of dirt while I worked along more slowly nearby. It occurred to me that what I had here was a once-in-a-lifetime chance to get to know Kel better and broaden my horizons, as Terri had suggested. Instead of just peering through my binoculars at the Reids and wondering why they were so weird, I should ask some intelligent questions and try to find out.

"Uh, I couldn't help noticing," I said, "that a lot of noise and commotion goes on at your house."

"It's a zoo, all right," he said, throwing a shovelful of dirt aside easily.

"Don't you ever wish you could have a little peace and quiet to think?"

"I have quiet when I'm out in the woods waiting for deer."

I was sorry I had asked. The very thought gave me the creeps—the poor little deer with their large, liquid eyes.

"It's really quiet there," he went on. "Not like home. Out in the woods it's so still you can hear the leaves drop."

I could see that would be different from his home. My guess was the only thing you could hear drop at the Reids' house was a bomb. As we kept on working, I realized it was amazing how all that shoveling warmed you up and tired you out. My arms were starting to feel heavy with weariness. In the past when I had seen vegetables and flowers springing miraculously out of the dirt, it was like hearing a chord of music or a line of poetry to me. It had never occurred to me that hours of backbreaking work and pounds of manure were essential to achieve the effect.

After a while Kel glanced at his watch and said, "I gotta go. I'm supposed to go skeet shooting with Bobby Manners at four-thirty."

I had never heard of a skeet. I supposed it must be some nocturnal animal if they were setting out so late. I cringed from finding out more about the various slaughters Kel engaged in, but I thought I might as well know the worst. "What's a skeet?" I asked.

He looked at me in surprise. "You know," he said, "when you shoot clay pigeons, that's shooting skeets."

"Clay pigeons?"

"Just a minute," he said. "I think I've got one in the garage somewhere." He leaped over the fence and soon returned with a dull-looking unglazed saucer.

"That's a clay pigeon?" I said incredulously.

He turned it over, looking at it. "I guess it's a funny name. I don't know why they're called that."

"I think shooting those things is a good idea," I said enthusiastically. "Why don't you shoot skeets all the time?"

"What is this thing you've got about hunting, Corrie?" Kel asked. "People have hunted forever, you know. You act as if it's immoral or something."

"Everything wants to live," I said.

"But everything's got to die," he said. "Whether I kill an animal or not, everything's got to die and mostly in worse ways than getting shot."

"I'll have to keep that in mind," I muttered, "if I ever get the urge to murder."

I don't think he heard me. He looked at his watch again and said, "I've got to go." He ran off, leaving his shovel against the fence. I could see that Bobby's car was driving up Kel's family's driveway. In a couple of minutes, Kel came charging out of his house carrying a shotgun, and he and Bobby drove off.

Listlessly, I shoveled some more, but it was boring work without Kel there to argue with and pretty soon I gave up on it and went inside. I ought to be nicer to him. Why did I always have to keep bringing up hunting? Nothing I said was going to stop the Reid boys from hunting. Why couldn't I be civil? But the thing was, I realized, I couldn't because there were things about Kel that I liked. It was a funny thing to realize, but I knew it was true. He obviously had a good heart—look at how he'd asked about my sniffles and helped me dig my garden. And I liked listening to him talk. Strong, silent types are boring. Even that cool, unwavering gaze of his wasn't so unnerving when you got used to it. I realized now that it was just the way he paid attention to things. I could see that a person could develop a fondness for having him around. In fact, it crossed my mind that if he weren't a bloodthirsty stalker of little animals and a crazy gun nut, I could probably like him a lot.

Saturday I wasn't able to do as much in the garden as I would have liked because that was the day of the double date with Terri and Eric, and I had to quit work early to get bathed and dressed. I had been dreading the evening so much I almost figured it couldn't be as bad as I had been imagining. But I was wrong. It was bad, all right.

Eric, Terri, and Marshall were all in Eric's old car when they stopped off at my house to get me. Marshall came up to the front door for me and we walked out to the car together. It suddenly hit me that Marshall must blow-dry his hair. That had to be how he got that fluffy, backswept look over the ears. Not that there's anything wrong with blow-drying your hair. I do it myself. But it was hard for me to visualize Marshall doing it. Did Kel do it? I wondered. No, probably he just slicked his down with bear grease or something. As I walked beside Marshall I couldn't resist sneaking little glances at his straw-colored hair. It was swept back at the temples with a touch of controlled curl. If my hair had looked that good I would have been delighted. As he opened the car door for me, I caught a faint whiff of hair spray! Well, I'll be darned, I thought. No wonder his hair always looked so neat.

"Hi, Corrie," Terri said, giving me a grateful look as I slid in.

Eric swung around to speak to Marshall and me. He had low, bushy eyebrows and a chin as big and broad as a shovel. "Why don't we go out on Ghost Point and see if we can find any ghosts?" he rumbled.

Anybody who would go out to Ghost Point with him should have her head examined, I thought. His was not a face you wanted to meet in the dark. "I think a movie would be more fun," I said firmly.

"Oh, I think so too," said Terri. "Let's go to a movie."

"Okay," grumbled Eric, "but there's never anything on in this dumb town."

"What about *Death in Sicily?*" suggested Marshall. "That's on at North Hills."

Eric looked at him incredulously. "Are you crazy? That's got *subtitles!*"

"What about *Marnie Meets Dracula?*" suggested Terri. "That might be fun."

Eric stepped on the gas and the car shot forward. "Okay by me," he growled, putting his arm around Terri. "As long as I can sit next to my woman."

I had to cling to the arm rest as we went around a corner, but when we hit the straightaway again I tried to talk to Marshall. "What did you think of that chemistry test?" I asked.

"I guess I did okay," he said indifferently.

The problem with Marshall was that he wasn't really interested in anything but skiing and money. And whenever I said anything he looked at me with that dead-fish expression that made the words die in my mouth. I heard a grating sound from the front seat and realized that Eric was trying to sing.

"It's you and me, babe," he rasped, looking down on Terri. "Through eternity, babe," he sang, making a futile attempt at a high note.

"Watch out for that bicycle," I gasped.

Eric neatly turned aside and missed the bicycle. I gulped. When I recovered from the shock I gathered myself together for another pitiful stab at conversation with Marshall. "I think those chemistry tests are getting easier," I said.

"Maybe so," said Marshall.

Meanwhile Eric warbled on in the front seat, sounding like a tractor trying to go uphill. "You are my desti-nee, babe," he sang. "Come and make me free, babe."

Terri was looking at him worshipfully. "Can you believe that Eric composed that song himself, Corrie?" she breathed.

"I can believe it," I said. "Uh, I guess you're thinking about college a lot these days, huh, Eric?" I thought it would be good to try to involve Eric in conversation. If nothing else, it would at least save us from the second verse of his song.

"I'm hoping I'll get into State," he said. "I want to be a dentist."

I glanced at his hands on the steering wheel—blunt, hairy hands that looked as if they'd been designed to stop a bayonet charge. I shuddered.

"That's wonderful," said Terri, starry-eyed. "To want to help people."

"You can make a lot of money that way too," said Marshall, nothing if not predictable.

Soon we pulled up to the Cardinal Theatre, a new place not far from our neighborhood. Inside, kids were crowded around, scuffing its fresh carpeting, waiting for the feature to start. "How about some popcorn, girls?" Eric growled as we joined the end of the line at the concession stand. I found myself thinking that Eric seemed to be nice enough. I shouldn't be prejudiced against people just because they had a face like a Mack truck and a voice like a rotary lawn mower. Just then I saw Kel making his way through the crowd carrying an overfilled cup of buttered popcorn. It was too late to hide. In a panic I thought of Mom's warning that if somebody sees you twice with the same guy they think you're going steady. Could I pretend to be with Eric? But Terri was clinging to Eric's arm as if the lobby were a ship starting to sink. Kel saw me, his steady eyes taking it all in. Just then, Marshall, with his talent for doing the wrong thing, put his hand on my waist. I quickly pulled away from him.

"Hi, Corrie," said Kel coolly, nodding to me. "Marshall."

I could feel myself going red, but Kel passed us and headed into the theatre. I wished I were dead. Marshall, on the other hand, looked almost cheerful. His eyes lit up with the first animation I could ever remember seeing in them. "Do you like your popcorn with butter?" he whispered in my ear.

"I think I'll just skip the popcorn," I said. I felt as if I would never want to eat again.

As soon as I got back home after the movie I closed the door behind me and leaned on it, relieved that the evening was over. Mom looked up as I came in. "Don't tell me," she said. "Let me guess. You're never going out with Marshall again."

"Boy, you said it!" I said fervently.

The next day I went over to Terri's and listened to her rhapsodize about Eric. For a long time I didn't say anything, but finally I chimed in with something that was bothering me. "Terri," I asked, "what makes Marshall go out with me? He's got to see that I can't stand him."

"That's easy," said Terri. "Marshall likes to be seen with a nice-looking girl on his arm. Didn't you notice how he perked up when Kel came by? It's not that he wants to go out with you as much as he wants people to see him going out with you."

"Well, that's good," I said doubtfully. "For a minute there I was afraid he might like me for myself."

"No danger," said Terri. "Honestly, Corrie, don't you think Eric is super? I mean, give me your honest opinion."

"He seems to be perfectly okay," I said. "He's nothing like as fierce as he looks."

"I'm so happy." Terri sighed.

I was happy about one thing, anyway. Now that Terri had broken the ice with Eric, she wouldn't be needing me to double-date with her anymore. I could concentrate on my schoolwork and my garden. I didn't expect any more help would be forthcoming from Kel. He was probably concluding that what I liked was boys like Marshall who used hair spray and talked about money all the time.

5

At last I was finally getting to the really interesting part of the work in the garden. I had already dug in every soil enricher that could be dug in and had all but pulverized the dirt to get it well blended. The time had come for me to put out the seedlings I had been growing so carefully under lights. I had germinated too many seedlings, but I couldn't bear to throw any of them away. I figured I would just plant them a little close together and thin them out later as I needed to once I saw which ones were the strongest.

As I came up to the garden I could see that Kel was out in his backyard. He had one foot propped up on a bench and was cleaning a gun with some brushes and old rags. The pale spring sunlight gleamed on his hair. He didn't turn around as I got to the garden, though. What a mistake it had been for me to go out with Marshall, I thought. I couldn't seem to do anything right. I let out a tiny sigh and put my trays of seedlings down beside the garden. Then all at once, I saw that the seedlings I had just planted the day before had vanished. I caught my breath sharply, feeling a little dizzy. What was going on? I had planted them and now they were gone!

I got down on my hands and knees and looked incredulously at the dirt. Then I saw that the seedlings were still there, but they had been trampled flat! "My seedlings!" I cried. "My precious little seedlings! Oh, no!"

"Corrie?" Kel called from the fence. "Anything wrong?"

I looked up. "Everything's wrong!" I cried. "My seedlings are all trampled."

Kel leaped over the fence and came to stand beside me to look at them. I found myself looking suspiciously at his feet. He was wearing his favorite boots with a chevron pattern of indentations on the sole. It wasn't those boots that had crushed the seedlings, I could see that. The stomper had been wearing some sort of tennis shoe.

Kel was looking at the damage with a faintly puzzled expression. He knelt down beside me. "Why would anybody want to do it?" he said.

"Maybe it was an accident," I said uncertainly.

"No way. There's a fence around the yard. Besides, look around. There aren't any footprints on the other side of the garden where nothing's been planted yet, but right here it looks as if some tribe has been doing the rain dance."

I looked at my pathetic, broken seedlings and sniffled. I

felt like a mother who has sent her six-year-old off to school the first day only to have him mugged. I pushed the hair out of my face. "What am I going to do?" I said desperately. "I have more seedlings. I have almost enough left, really, to fill the whole garden, but if this happens again I'll be wiped out. It will be too late for me to grow more seeds before the date the project is due."

"Tell you what," he said. "There's a full moon tonight. A hunter's moon, they call it," he went on, looking at me sideways. "Why don't I keep watch over the garden tonight from my bedroom? Up on the second story there I've got a clear view of the garden."

"Oh, I couldn't let you do that," I said. "It's not your problem. Besides, you can't keep watch like that every night."

"Maybe we'll think up something else by tomorrow," said Kel. "I'd get a kick out of it. I'd love to catch the stinker. Good grief, think of all the digging we put in on this blinking garden. Who does he think he is?"

His eyes were glowing with anticipation. It hit me that for Kel stalking the stomper would be a superior kind of hunting. It seemed almost indecent the way he was enjoying it all, but I knew it was lucky for me that he was willing to help out. I wanted to catch the guy who had done in my plants too.

I got up off the ground and dusted off my knees. "If you'd like to do that, it would be a big help to me," I said. "I can't see the garden at all from my window."

I set about putting out my new plants, trying hard not to think about the ones that had been trampled. As I worked I could hear Kel whistling in his backyard while he cleaned his gun. I guess he was already looking forward to the adventure of finding the seedling stomper. I wished I had his confidence. As I patted the dirt around the roots of the last set of tiny plants, my fingers were almost trembling. I was worried. How long did it take to trample seedlings, after all? Wasn't it possible we wouldn't catch the stomper in time to save the plants?

Later, after I had picked up and put away all my empty plastic flower pots and seedling flats in the tool shed, I saw that Kel was up at Miss Addie's front gate working on it with a screwdriver. I followed him up there. "What are you doing?" I asked.

He didn't say anything but slowly opened the gate. It screeched as the hinges moved. "I'm unfixing it," he grinned. "I could use a little advance warning if the prowler shows up tonight, and a good screech from the gate will help. I'm going to do the same thing to the side gate."

"But you won't be able to hear a squeak from this gate way over at your house," I pointed out.

"I know," he said, pocketing the screwdriver. "That's why you'd better keep your window open tonight and listen out for it. If you hear it open, call me up right away."

My heart began to pound faster at the thought. I could see it was going to take quick work on my part to get to the phone and call Kel in time for him to do anything. I began to hope the prowler would choose the side gate, the one closest to Kel's house.

After I went back into the house, I had to admit to

myself that being in on a chase was exciting in a way. It certainly beat just sitting by the garden with tears running down my face. Here, at least, was something I could do about the problem.

That night I put on a warm sweater and sat by my window with a book. I had the shades pulled down because I didn't want to scare off the intruder if he were coming by the front way, but I left a four-inch crack open at the bottom so I could hear the first screech of the gate.

"Corrie," Mom called. "Can you come help me pin this skirt?"

I went to the door of my bedroom and called softly, "Not now, Mom, I'm trying to catch a prowler."

Mom instantly appeared at my door. "What did you say, Corinda?"

I eyed my window nervously, wishing I was sitting at my post. "Kel and I are keeping watch tonight from our windows to make sure my new seedlings don't get stomped on."

"Just what are you going to do if you catch this prowler?" said Mom, looking alarmed.

"Uh, scare him away, I guess," I said lamely. Kel and I hadn't exactly gone into that. "Look, Mom, I'm supposed to be at my window, listening."

"All right," she said. "I don't suppose there's any harm in sitting by your window, but don't you get any ideas about going outside and chasing this person, do you hear?"

"He probably won't even show up again," I said impatiently. I was anxious to get back to my station.

"Just remember what I said," Mom said.

"Okay," I said. "I'll remember. I don't want to go chasing him anyway."

"Good," said Mom.

Just as I was walking back to my post, I thought I heard a squeaking sound. But it was very faint. Maybe it was my imagination. I knelt and peered desperately out the crack in my window. It was amazing how hard it was to see out there when your eyes weren't used to the dark. There were so many shadows. I could make out the ghostly white palings of Miss Addie's fence and her front gate. The only thing that seemed to be moving, though, was the shadows of the trees in the night wind.

Suddenly I heard a cry at the other end of the yard, like that of an animal, maybe a screech owl. I was so edgy my knuckles were white as I gripped the windowsill. I peered nervously out the window. Then and there I forgot my promise to Mom to stay put. I wanted to get outside and see what was going on. I swiftly ran downstairs to the kitchen. Maybe I could just stand on the stoop and see if I could get a better view from there. I had to know what was going on.

"Corinda!" Mom's voice pursued me down the stairs.

All at once the phone rang, practically at my ear, in the kitchen. I snatched up the receiver. "Hello," I gasped.

"Corrie? It's Kel. I got him! I hit him square on."

I leaned weakly against the kitchen wall. "Kel," I said, my voice quavering. "You didn't shoot him did you?"

I was relieved that he sounded appalled. "Good grief," he said, "what do you think I am?"

"I guess I just freaked out for a moment," I said apologetically, feeling weak with relief. "But if you didn't shoot him, how did you hit him?"

"With my slingshot," he said. "You should have heard him yell!"

"I think I did," I said.

"He took off like a bat out of a hot place," he said. "He never knew what hit him. He won't be stomping on any seedlings tonight."

Kel sounded smug, but then, he had a right to be. "Who was it?" I asked him. "Did you see?"

"No such luck," he said. "You know what the light's like out there. I couldn't pick him out of a lineup, that's for sure."

"Blond or brunette?"

"I can't say," he said. "I don't think the light was ever on his face. It was just a body in the shadows. I couldn't even judge his height from where I was."

After I hung up I saw that Mom and Dad had been standing at the kitchen door waiting for me to get off the phone. "Would you kindly tell us, Corrie," Dad said, "what in the name of heaven is going on?"

"Kel got the guy who's been stomping on my garden. Hit him with his slingshot," I said. "He was watching for him to show up and when he did—wham! The guy took off running, though, and Kel didn't see who it was."

"How very odd," Mom said, her brow furrowed. "Why would anybody want to ruin your vegetable garden?"

"I don't know. It's weird, all right."

"Probably just some kid's idea of a good time," Dad said.

"Some idea of a good time!" I said. "Somebody who gets his kicks stomping on lettuce sprouts has got to be truly warped."

"I don't know," said Dad. "Look at kids who go smashing pumpkins all over town at Halloween. Look at kids who like to wrap toilet paper around somebody's house. This isn't any stranger than that."

I felt doubtful. It still seemed to me that stomping on tiny little plants was a different sort of thing.

"We'd better get to bed," Mom said. "Look at the time."

Even when I did go upstairs and get into bed, I couldn't get to sleep. I kept trying to think up traps we could set for the intruder. Now that he had been back twice, it was hard to imagine he was going to give up. At least, I wasn't willing to bet my seedlings on it.

The next day I went out to examine the scene of the crime. There were no tracks on the thick matted grass, of course, but there was a familiar tennis-shoe print at the edge of the garden. Kel had hit him with the slingshot just in time. When Kel appeared I showed him the footprint. He knelt down and gloated. "See this skid and the way the toe is dug in?" he said. "That must be when I hit him." He cast a look at the second story of his house. "Not a bad shot," he said. "That's my bedroom on the end there."

I looked over at the house and saw at once which window was Kel's. He had taken the screen off so as to be able to use his slingshot. "That's a long way," I said.

"Let's face it," he said. "I really have a good eye."

"You wouldn't be a little vain about it, would you?" I asked.

"Okay, I'm vain." He grinned. "You can see yourself it was a tricky shot—a moving target, in moonlight, and from that distance."

"Oh, I admit it," I said. "What I'm worrying about is where we go from here. "What's to stop this guy from coming back? We can't spend every night watching the garden. We need to rig up some sort of trap."

"I've got it all figured out," he said, rubbing his hands together. "I'm going to run a few lines of electrical wires around the garden low down."

"Won't that be dangerous?" I said.

"They won't have a strong charge," he said. "It'll be just like those things people run around the tops of fences to keep their dogs from jumping out."

"I don't see how that will work. So he steps on an electrical wire. With tennis shoes on he won't feel a thing."

"But that's only the beginning," Kel said. "Stepping on the wires will break the circuit and then a buzzer will go off in my house. I have it all figured out." He took a pencil out of his pants pocket to sketch a diagram for me, but I said quickly, "That's okay. I'll just take your word for it."

I would have liked to have the buzzer go off in my house, but since my mom and dad had made it clear I wasn't to budge a step out of the house looking for any prowler, there wouldn't be anything I could do even if the alarm did go off. There was nothing to do but agree to rig it up to Kel's house.

Kel looked speculatively back toward his house. "I wonder if I could rig it up to set off the carillon," he said. "That would really scare him, I bet."

"I think the buzzer would be better," I said. One of the few ways the neighborhood had been quieter since the Reids had taken over the Harrisons' house was that the Reids didn't play the carillon. We were all grateful for that. It hadn't been so bad when the Harrisons played "Hark the Herald Angels Sing" around Christmas time, and I don't think anybody minded "Love Makes the World Go Round" on Valentine's Day, but when it got to the point when the evening news was just about drowned out every night by taps, there had been a lot of talk of calling the police. "Some people complain about the noise of the carillon," I explained.

"A buzzer would be easier, anyway," Kel admitted. I could see he would have loved nothing better than to plan a full-scale manhunt complete with bloodhounds, helicopters, and searchlights.

"Let's keep it simple," I said.

When I came out the next afternoon to do some mulching I found that Kel had wasted no time getting the alarm set up. He had already put up several lines of electrical wires, set just slightly above the ground and going around the garden. You could barely make out the dark wires against the garden dirt.

"The only thing is," he said, driving in a stake to support the last line of wire, "You're going to have to be careful not to step on it yourself or you'll set off the alarm."

I looked at the wires distrustfully. "What if a robin steps on one?" I asked. "What happens to the poor robin?"

"It's a very weak charge," Kel said impatiently. "Besides, if the robin actually perches on the wire he won't be grounded."

"I hope you're right."

"I'm right," he said. "Now, another thing. Don't let a shovel or anything fall on this or it will tear the whole thing apart. And don't mention it to anybody. After all, the stomper is almost bound to be somebody from right around here. Nobody else would even know that you had a garden."

I thought about that for a while and decided I'd rather not. It was awful to start getting suspicious of people. I've never been one of those people who wants to live a thrilling life the way people on TV shows do, spying on people and living dangerously. I'm a person who likes simple, quiet pleasures. I did not want to set up alarm systems to trap prowlers. The problem was, I didn't have much choice. If I wanted to save my seedlings and have any hope of passing home ec, I was going to have to fight back. I sighed. "I think you'd better disconnect the thing during the day," I said. "I'm bound to knock against it when I'm putting out mulch or whatever."

"Okay," he agreed reluctantly. "But promise me you won't go dumping junk on it. It was hard enough to get it put up in the first place."

I promised. Later on, when I finished mulching and went inside, I reflected again that I was really lucky I had

Kel to help me in my fight against the seedling stomper. After all, I couldn't do much better for help than a guy who had dead aim with a slingshot and who, besides, was handy at rigging burglar alarms. Another nice thing about Kel as a helper was that he had a confident air that made me feel we were actually going to catch that stomper.

6

The next day Terri and I went to the ice cream shop at the mall after school. We took our snacks to a quiet table where I could fill her in on Kel's and my pursuit of the seedling stomper.

"You really think it's somebody in the neighborhood?" Terri asked, taking a sip of diet drink.

"Who else would even know about the garden?"

"Somebody in the neighborhood could have leaked the information."

"I don't think so," I said. "It's not as if my planting a garden were a juicy bit of gossip. Why would anybody mention it to anyone else?"

"Maybe you're right," Terri conceded. "But even if you limit it to someone in your neighborhood, that doesn't narrow it down much."

"I know," I said, digging into the whipped cream on my sundae.

Terri leaned over the table. "Have you ever thought that Kel might be the one who's doing it?" she hissed.

"I know that's the way it always is in detective movies," I said, attacking a scoop of chocolate ice cream, "but I don't see how it could be. For one thing, I've never seen him in tennis shoes, have you?"

"Maybe that's just the point," said Terri. "Maybe to throw you off the trail he bought some tennis shoes."

"No," I said. "It doesn't make sense. It must have taken him hours to set up that electrical burglar alarm system. You should see it. I mean, you'd have to be absolutely cuckoo to go to all that trouble just for a sick practical joke."

"But maybe there's some other motive," Terri said. "Maybe he's fallen for you and wants to have an excuse to hang around and get to know you better." She leaned closer to me. "These are primitive emotions, Corrie."

"You've been paying too much attention to Eric's songs," I said, "if Kel wanted to see more of me it would be easier for him to ask me out for a sundae or something. It's got to be somebody else who's doing it." I gave a little sigh as I spooned up another bite of ice cream. "Believe me, I'd like to think Kel wanted to see me that much," I said, "but there's not a chance of it."

"Gotten to where you kind of like him, huh?" said Terri.

I was glad that she didn't rub it in about how I had changed my tune about Kel. "Yup," I said. "Now that

I'm up against a mad seedling stomper, I've begun to really appreciate Kel—his handiness with a screwdriver, his aim with a slingshot. . . ."

"Sounds like a wonderful basis for a relationship," said Terri. "I wonder if I could have just a teensie eensie little bite of that banana split?"

I pushed it across to her. "I don't think we're going to have much of a relationship," I said sadly. "Not a romantic one, anyway. He's just not interested. But at least I have his help as a fellow detective, which is not to be sneezed at. Tell me," I said kindly, "how is it going with you and Eric?" With my own romantic life such a wreck, I noticed within myself stirrings of a desire to be a better person, to be more kind and considerate to others. I supposed it was the same state of mind that made people with blighted romances join convents or the French Foreign Legion.

There was a long silence from Terri.

"Is everything okay?" I asked.

"Oh, I guess so," said Terri. "But you know, Eric hasn't turned out to be at all the way I expected."

"Gee, that's too bad," I said sympathetically.

"He's a fairly ordinary kind of guy, and he talks a lot about dental school," she said. Then she burst out, "Joe and I used to have such good talks."

I looked around the shop nervously to make sure that neither Joe nor Eric had come in, as this was beginning to look fairly messy even with no further complications. "Uh, exactly how did you break off with Joe?" I asked, seeing at once that this might be critical under the circumstances.

"I said I thought we both needed more room to grow," Terri said glumly.

That didn't sound too bad. "And?" I asked.

"And I hear he's growing with Suzy Stinette," said Terri, her eyes brimming.

To my surprise, I didn't have the slightest desire to say, "I told you so." Poor Terri, I thought. She's blown it.

As soon as I got home from the ice cream shop I changed into old clothes and went out to work in the garden. I was working there almost every day now. It was amazing how quickly weeds sprang up. Where did they all come from? And it seemed like no time until bugs began to appear. I spent a lot of time down on my hands and knees peering at them unhappily and wondering what to do about them. Somehow I didn't quite like the idea of poisoning them or squashing them. So far, I had to admit, the actual experience of growing a garden was turning out more the way it was described in the gardening books and less and less the way it was described in the seed catalogues. There were lots of bugs and plenty of dirt. The only good thing was that there was no sign of the seedling stomper. It began to look as if he had given up. I even started to think of asking Kel to take away the burglar alarm. It was a terrible pain to keep from knocking it down when I was gardening. Then, all of a sudden late that night, the phone rang. It was Kel. "We've had a visitor again," he said glumly.

"Did he do any damage?" I asked, my heart in my mouth.

"Yup," Kel said. "I was just out there with a flashlight, checking."

I sat down on the kitchen stool, my grip on the telephone loosening a little. I imagined a scene of utter carnage and destruction among the cabbages.

"I wish I had gotten him with the slingshot again," Kel said.

"You mean you missed?"

"Of course I didn't miss," he said. "I tried to run after him and catch him, but I was too far away even to come close. It was a dumb idea. He heard me coming and took off."

I tried to calculate how much damage the stomper could do between the time the buzzer went off in Kel's bedroom and the time he could get downstairs and out into the backyard. "I've got to see the garden," I said suddenly. "I'm going out there with a flashlight right now."

"I'll meet you back there," said Kel.

I was sure Mom and Dad wouldn't like me being on the tracks of the intruder, but luckily they were engrossed in a movie on television upstairs and wouldn't have heard the house falling down. I quietly threw on my quilted bathrobe over my pajamas and crept out the back door carrying our big flashlight. I moved quietly down the back steps and onto the grass. The flashlight cast a weak circle of light in the blackness, seeming to magnify whatever it fell on. As I moved the light, the shadows of bushes seemed to rear up at me. Even the blades of grass cast long shadows. It was a very dark night with no moon, and it didn't take much imagination to suppose that the prowler was creeping along beside me, out of reach of the flashlight. I began to wish I was back in my bed. I turned the flashlight beam ahead of me and found the gate at the back of the yard. The dew on the grass was seeping through my nylon slippers. My toes were cold. If I hadn't told Kel I would meet him, I would have turned around and gone back to the house, but I didn't want him to know what a chicken I was.

I heard a noise far to the right and almost dropped the flashlight in a panic, but then I saw the glow of a light and realized it was only Kel making his way back to the garden. I moved carefully through our back gate and turned toward the garden, hurrying now as fast as I could. As I approached, Kel called to me, "Be careful where you step. You don't want to wipe out any footprints he might have made." It was amazing how much braver I felt once I was standing beside Kel at the garden and there were two flashlights shining into the blackness instead of one. I shone mine onto the garden. As my light approached the edge of the garden I saw signs of destruction. I walked closer and shone the light on the broken stalks and the bruised leaves trampled into the dirt. "Lucky I started out with a big garden," I said grimly. "That way I still have some left."

Kel came to stand beside me and shone his flashlight on the garden. "You know," he said, "I can't figure out why anybody would want to do this."

"I just hope we're not adding to the excitement of it for the creep by trying to catch him at it."

"Well, if he wants excitement," said Kel, sounding almost like a disembodied voice in the darkness, "he'll get it. Tomorrow night I'm going to camp out here and catch him."

"Don't you think that's going a little far?" I said.

"Any other ideas?"

I would have loved to come up with some plan—incisive, brilliant, and daring—but I couldn't think of a thing. "I'd better get back inside," I said. "I don't want my parents to send out a search party." I felt as if I would like to say something encouraging, Kel seemed so down, but I couldn't think of anything. "I don't think it's such a good idea for you to camp out back here," I said. "Think about it for a minute. The kind of warped mind that would stomp on little seedlings—do you want to meet this guy in the dark?"

I saw Kel's teeth flash white in the faint reflection from his flashlight. "Yes," he said.

"Maybe you'd better talk it over with your parents first."

"Oh, I don't think they'll mind," he said, sounding amused.

I realized that, of course, the sort of parents that let their kids end up in the hospital from exposure would think nothing of letting them camp out in the backyard. It made me wonder about Kel's parents. "What does your father do for a living?" I asked suddenly.

Kel's teeth flashed again in the darkness. "Until he retired last year," Kel said, "he was a colonel in the Marines."

That settled that, I thought. I had never known a marine personally before, but if you could judge by what you saw in the movies, then I guessed when Kel told his folks he wanted to camp out to catch the prowler his father would give him a knife to hold in his teeth and offer to lay a few mines for him. I sighed. "What are you going to do if you catch him?" I asked.

"I'm not sure I'm going to try to catch him," Kel said. "I just want to shine a light right in his face and see who he is."

That sounded sensible at least, and it made me feel a bit better. A little later, when I got back to the house, I took off my slippers so as not to leave wet tracks when I tiptoed quietly upstairs. All I was hoping was that Kel didn't get himself clobbered while tracking the stomper.

The next night, Saturday, Kel took his sleeping bag out to Miss Addie's yard as he had planned. I got a play-by-play account of his movements from Tim. It seemed that Kel's brothers were offering technical advice and following the whole thing with intense interest. "Kel's back there now," Tim said, when he hung up after talking to Jason. "He wrapped a cloth around his flashlight so it wouldn't be so bright while he was walking back there with the sleeping bag. Very sneaky."

"Does he have a tent?" I asked.

"Naw," said Tim. "His mom wanted him to take a pup tent, but his dad said it would only block his vision and slow him down."

"It doesn't sound very comfortable," I said.

"The Reid boys don't care about that," said Tim. "They're tough. Naturally, everybody wanted to go with him to help catch the guy, but Colonel Reid made 'em stay in. He said it was Kel's show."

I went to my room and peeked out the window, but it was a dark night and I might as well have been looking down the kitchen drain. After that, I tried to get down to my American history reading, but I couldn't keep my mind on it. I waited until after Tim went to bed and Mom and Dad were hooked on the Saturday-night TV movie; then I slipped out of my flimsy slippers and into loafers, went downstairs, grabbed the big flashlight, and headed out the back door. After a moment's hesitation, I also grabbed a kitchen towel and wrapped it around the flashlight to subdue the light.

With the flashlight wrapped up in the dishtowel, it was darker than ever going back to the garden, but it must be true that you can get used to anything, because this time going back there didn't bother me so much. I knew I had better not go too quietly or Kel might think I was the prowler and zap me with a slingshot or something, so as I turned toward the back of the lot I started calling softly, "Kel? Kel?"

Suddenly, at what seemed like practically my shoulder, Kel said, "Good grief, Corrie, what are you doing back here? What if I'd thought you were the stomper? Maybe you're scaring him off. Go back to the house."

"I'm not scaring him off any more than you did," I said. "There's no reason why you should be the only one to come back here. Show me where you're staying."

I followed him over to some bushes beside the back fence. "I've got my sleeping bag right here," he said. "Okay, now you've seen it. Now beat it back to the house. The guy may show up any minute."

"You seem to want to hog all the excitement," I said.

"You sound like my brothers," said Kel. "Do you want to be the one to stake out the place?"

I thought about it a minute. Actually, I couldn't believe I had said that about him hogging the excitement. Me, who never wanted any excitement, just a good book and a warm fire. "No," I said. "I don't want to stake out the place. I was just checking on you. You don't need anything, do you?"

"I am an experienced woodsman," he said haughtily. "Naturally, I have planned this all carefully."

"I just hope you're not too cold," I said.

"I'll be okay," he said.

Kel could be extremely exasperating. I turned reluctantly back toward the house. When I got inside once more, I dried off my loafers and tiptoed up the stairs carrying them. As luck would have it, Mom with her bat-keen ears heard me tiptoeing past her room. "Corrie?" she called, coming to the door of her room. "Why do you have your loafers there?"

"Uh, I was thinking I would take them downstairs and polish them, but changed my mind."

"Corinda," Mom said, looking at me piercingly, "you haven't been out looking for that prowler, have you?"

"Oh, no," I said.

"Come on back, Margaret," called Dad. "You're missing it!"

"Just be sure you don't," said Mom. "It wouldn't be safe."

"I'm not chasing any prowlers," I said. And I hadn't been. In fact, I'd actually tried to persuade Kel not to sleep back there, hadn't I? I went to my room with an almost clear conscience.

I saw Kel at church the next morning. Except for Mrs.

Reid, who came very regularly, you didn't see the Reids at church much because they were usually out hunting on the weekends, so I wasn't looking for Kel. Add to that that I wasn't used to seeing him in a good suit and wearing a tie, and it isn't surprising that I almost didn't recognize him. But after the service, as the congregation filed out of the pews, I realized that he was right in front of me. That smooth, toffee-colored hair could belong to no one else. "Kel?" I said. At first he started to turn his head, but a cry of pain escaped him; he then, very cautiously and without moving his head, turned around until he was facing me. "Is something wrong?" I said, alarmed.

"No, I just got a stiff neck from sleeping out last night. I'm okay unless I try to look up . . . or down . . . or right or left."

"Oh, dear," I said. "Have you tried a hot-water bottle?"

"Yes," he said, gritting his teeth. "When I could have used the hot-water bottle was last night."

I knew this camping out back was a dumb idea, I thought, but I was tactful enough not to say it. "I've been thinking about our problem," I said, "and I think we'd better give up this camping out. I mean, you can't sleep out there every night." I lowered my voice in case the prowler should be standing nearby among the worshipers. "I think the thing to do is to rig up an alarm system connected to the gates. We could unhook it during the day so people like the meter reader wouldn't set it off accidentally. It could buzz in both our houses. Then when we hear it go off we can run out back and throw firecrackers to scare the prowler off."

I liked my idea. It was perfectly respectable and had the advantage of not leaving me inside wondering what was going on while Kel had all the fun. But Kel just looked at me with that familiar unblinking blue gaze and said coldly, "Don't you want to catch the stinker? I'm going to sleep back out there again tonight."

I knew what was the matter with him. He probably hadn't slept a wink last night so he was cross. And if he kept insisting on sleeping out on these damp, cool spring nights he was only going to get more and more cross. Plus he would end up so stiff that pretty soon you wouldn't be able to tell him from the Tin Woodman after a rainstorm. But I saw that the glint in his blue eyes was sheer wooden-headed stubbornness, so I didn't try to reason with him. "All right," I said meekly. Find out for yourself, I thought. Find out for yourself that this camping out is a dumb idea.

As it turned out though, I didn't get a chance to crow after all because that very night Kel sneaked up on the prowler and saw who it was. I found out about it Monday morning. When I saw Kel before school he backed me against the wall of the hall, leaned over me, and filled me in on the latest. "I saw him," he hissed.

"No!" I said, wide-eyed. "Did you recognize him?"

"Yes," he said, looking at me a little strangely. "It was Marshall."

The bell rang practically over my head. I covered my ears with my hands to protect my eardrums. "Marshall?" I said, wrinkling my nose. "I can't believe it."

"I didn't think you'd like it," said Kel.

Kids were streaming by us on their way to assembly, and I knew I needed to get going, but I was too stunned to move.

"Look," I said hotly, "if you think I have a thing about Marshall, you couldn't be more wrong. I only went to that movie with him as a favor to Terri. She needed somebody to double with. But I just can't see Marshall as a prowler. Are you sure, absolutely sure, that it was him?"

"What other boy do we know who has a bouffant hairdo?" asked Kel. "Besides, I called out his name and he jumped a mile."

"It might have been just the sound of your voice that startled whoever it was," I said dubiously, thinking of all I'd read about how unreliable eyewitness reports were. "Look, I've got to get to class. I'll think about what you said. But you've got to admit it doesn't sound very likely. I mean, what could his motive be? And really, does he strike you as the type?"

"Yes," said Kel positively. "He does."

I scooted out from under his arms and ran to assembly. When I filed into my row with my homeroom class, I saw that Marshall was three rows ahead of me. Mr. Milam, the principal, came to the microphone and introduced a special presentation called Safety at School, but I couldn't take my eyes off Marshall. I was trying to come to grips with what Kel had told me. Was it really possible, I asked myself, that Marshall was the prowler? Could I imagine him risking his expensive clothes prowling through Miss Addie's yard at night? Of course, even Marshall must have a pair of old jeans somewhere. Still, it was hard to imagine. With his sort of pinched-looking nose, his fluffy hair, and his bored look, he was more cut out to be a model in a store window than a prowler. Maybe Kel and I should confront Marshall and demand an explanation. I thought that was what we should do. He would probably just deny it. It was worth a try, though.

7

At lunch, the first thing I told Terri was that I had to find Kel.

"I saw you two in the hall this morning," she said. "It looked very cozy."

"Strictly business," I told her. "We've got a strong lead in the case of the seedling stomper."

Terri unwrapped her sandwich disconsolately. "I'm the one who wants adventure and you're the one who gets it," she said. "It's not fair. What kind of a lead?"

"Kel shone his flashlight right at the prowler last night, and he said it was Marshall."

Terri's mouth fell open. "No!" she managed to say finally. "Do you think Marshall knows how fed up you are with him and this is how he's getting back at you? He still burns with unrequited passion, you see, and he takes it out on your garden."

"Honestly, Terri, passion isn't the only motive in the world," I said testily.

"Hey, there's Kel," she said. "Over there."

I took a firm grip on my tray and got up to brave the crowd that crammed into the cafeteria at noon. I finally fought my way over to Kel's table.

"Hi, Corrie," he said.

I looked around the table packed with boys and said, "I need to talk to you about something—privately."

Kel looked around him helplessly. The cafeteria at high noon was no place for a private talk. "Just leave your tray here," he said. "We'll go up to the window."

I could feel the eyes of all the boys at Kel's table following us as we walked up front to the window where people push their trays into the kitchen when they finish eating. It was not exactly the beauty spot of the cafeteria, what with the spilled milk and the constant crash of trays beside us, but there was more privacy there. Kids rushed by us now and then to slam their trays in the window, but nobody hung around to eavesdrop.

"I think we ought to confront Marshall," I said in a hoarse whisper. "Tell him we're on to him and demand an explanation."

"I think you're right," Kel whispered back.

"Good," I said. "Then let's do it."

He grinned. "I have," he said. "I caught up with him after assembly and told him if I caught him anywhere near the garden again I was going to wring his worthless neck."

"What did he say?"

Kel shrugged. "Nothing. But he did turn kind of white. Then he took off. I don't think we're going to have any more trouble with him."

I knew how unsettling a look from Kel could be even when he wasn't threatening your life, and for a second I felt almost sorry for Marshall. "I hope you're right," I said. "I can't imagine why Marshall would do this, but if he stops doing it, that's all I care about."

When I went back to Kel's table to retrieve my tray, I felt very conspicuous. All the boys looked at me with intense interest. I managed a nervous little smile at them, grabbed my tray, and headed back to Terri. She was already finished eating by the time I got back to our table, but she had stayed on, waiting for me.

"Whew," I said. "I haven't had a chance to eat a bite. Kel's table was packed, and we had to go up front to get a little privacy to talk."

"I saw," said Terri. "Everybody saw. You could almost see people taking notes all over the cafeteria—Kel and Corrie: Hot item."

The thought of it made me feel a little uncomfortable, as if I were using a fake I.D. card or something, but there was no help for it. I didn't think I could very well tell everybody in the school about Marshall. Even if I didn't mind blackening his reputation I had the idea that lots of people might think being plagued by a seedling stomper was kind of funny, and I didn't much like the thought of people laughing at my problem. "Kel already had a showdown with Marshall and threatened him if he came near the garden again," I said.

"Good."

"I don't think I approve of it on moral grounds," I said, "but I sure hope it works."

"What did Marshall say?"

"Nothing. Kel said he just turned white."

"Ooo, I can just see it," said Terri. "You are so lucky to have Kel to help you out with all this."

"He's a very efficient partner," I said. "Kind of ruthless, but efficient."

"I didn't mean just that," said Terri. "It's all that good propinquity you've got going for you."

"What?"

"Propinquity," she said. "Being around somebody a lot. It's a well-known scientific fact that boys mostly fall for girls that they're around a lot. How did your parents meet, for example."

"At a New Year's Eve party."

"The theory doesn't work in 100% of the cases, of course," she said hastily. "But the fact is that most boys fall for the girl next door. Don't you see?"

"What I don't see is the slightest sign of it," I said. "In fact, now that we've caught Marshall, I expect I won't be seeing any more of Kel. He'll be off hunting rabbits or something now."

Just then Marshall walked in the cafeteria door. I quickly looked down at my meat loaf. This was embarrassing. It was an awkward social situation. Was I supposed to give a friendly hello to someone who was trying to destroy my garden and have me fail home ec? I avoided the problem by studying my peas and meat loaf. A minute later, though, I became aware that someone was almost leaning over me. I looked up and for one time in my life was relieved to see that it was only Otis Boggs.

Terri at once grabbed her brown paper bag and hopped up. "I've got to go. I'll be late for class. 'Bye, Corrie. 'Bye, Otis." Otis slid into Terri's chair and gave me a big smile, which bared all thirty-two ivory teeth. Whatever else you could say about Otis, you had to admit that he was bound to get a good dental checkup. "I hear you've been having some trouble in home economics," he drawled. "I'm sorry to hear that. I hope this little problem you're having won't adversely affect your grade average."

I gave him a warm smile. "You're sweet to be so concerned, Otis. You really are."

"Well, I am concerned, Corrie. Sincerely concerned."

I'll bet you are, I thought to myself. I could almost feel the wheels of Otis's agile brain computing how much of a dent home economics, an unweighted, nonacademic course, could make in my average. "Home ec has given me a bad time," I said sweetly, "but I think I may now have it all under control."

"I'm very glad to hear that, Corrie," he drawled. "Very glad indeed. I can't tell you."

"I know," I said, demurely lowering my lashes. "Well, I must run."

As I dumped my scarcely touched tray into the tray window with a satisfying crash, it crossed my mind to wonder whether Marshall was Otis's paid agent. After all, I wouldn't put it past Marshall to do anything for money. But as I passed by Otis again on my way out of the cafeteria and he flashed me his enormous set of teeth, I realized that all this melodrama and sneaking around in gardens at night was probably beginning to affect my mind. Otis might not be Mr. Charm and he might want to be at the top of the class, but it was ridiculous to think he'd stoop to vandalism. After all, I wanted to be at the top myself, and I didn't go putting knock-out drops into Otis's milk. Not that it wouldn't be a pleasure, I thought, giving him a friendly wave as I went out the door.

After the day that Kel confronted Marshall face-to-face, the alarm system remained silent. As April moved along, the banks turned purple with broad blankets of thrift. Tulips swayed gently in the breeze, and the white canopy of dogwood flowers burst forth. Less glamorous, but even better from my point of view, my cabbages, lettuces, and radishes were ripening. Soon I would be able to take my first basket of vegetables in to class. Altogether now, things were going just the way I wanted them to. Kel was off a lot shooting with his brothers while I peacefully hoed my garden. I had to admit, though, that life was a little dull. I missed Kel. I even almost missed the struggle with the stomper.

One kind of strange thing happened, though, just as I was carefully hoeing the cabbages. I looked up and saw a station wagon pulling up in front of Miss Addie's house. Marshall got out of it and headed toward the house. He was wearing a sports jacket and looked like an Easter ad for a men's clothing store. He opened the gate and it let out a loud screech. He looked at it uneasily; then, leaving it ajar, he went on up the walk to the house. At first I wondered what on earth he was up to, but then I remembered he was supposed to be keeping an eye on the place for Miss Addie. It made me nervous to have him come within a quarter mile of my vegetables, but he must only have been doing the job she was paying him for.

Even after I finished hoeing the broccoli, I hung around to keep an eye on what he was doing, and about ten minutes later he came out again. He went up the front walk carrying a chair, one of those plain wooden chairs with arms and a back made of spokes. He sat it down on the sidewalk while he opened the gate a little wider, then carried it to the car. The fence blocked my view a little, but I could see he seemed to be wrapping cloth around its back legs. He opened the tailgate of the station wagon and slowly laid the chair on its back there. He was certainly being very careful with it. Then he got in the car and drove off.

Just then I heard a thwacking noise and saw that Kel was sitting on his family's back stoop knocking mud off his boots. He was wearing a baggy camouflage outfit all covered with liver-shaped olive and brown spots and splattered with mud. In fact, it looked a little as if he had been crawling along on his stomach. I had a passing pang of sympathy for his poor mother, who was going to have to wash his clothes. I leaned against the fence and called to him. "Kel?" I said. "Kel?"

He looked up and quickly came over to the fence. The contrast between Marshall's fashionable sleek pants and sports coat couldn't have been more complete, but somehow in spite of it, Kel looked better to me. "Any trouble?" he said.

"I guess not," I said slowly. "But the funniest thing happened just now. Marshall came out of Miss Addie's house with a chair and then just drove off with it."

Kel looked over toward Miss Addie's house, his eyes narrowing. "But that's burglary," he said. "You mean he did that in broad daylight with you watching him? He must be nuts."

"I think he's got a key to the house," I said. "Miss Addie's paying him to keep an eye on it. What I don't understand is why he was taking that chair out. Doesn't it seem a little bit odd to you?"

"I'll say."

"Maybe he's taking it home to polish it or something. You know, Marshall's family is in the furniture business. He might notice that something like that needed doing before most people would."

"Baloney," said Kel. "He would have polished it on the spot. Or if it was going to make a mess, he could have taken it out in the backyard to do it."

"There's probably some perfectly innocent explanation for all this," I said.

Kel looked at me with pity. "There's some explanation for it, all right," he said. "But you can bet it's not innocent. You're just too trusting, Corrie."

I felt stung. First Terri had told me I had a marshmallow heart, and now Kel was saying I was too trusting. I can be as hardboiled as the next guy, I thought. "I'll certainly keep an eye out to make sure he returns the chair," I said. "You can bet on that."

"Good," said Kel, looking thoughtfully in the direction of the big house.

I kept a very close eye on the house after that. When I was working out in the garden, that was easy, but I also started studying near my bedroom window just to keep an eye out. A few days later my close watch paid off. The front gate alerted me with its fearful shriek and I looked out my window to see Marshall edging through the gate, holding it open with one foot while he carried the chair through. How about that, I thought. He really had been planning to bring it back all the time. Kel was wrong about him stealing it.

I dashed quickly downstairs and out the back door. I snatched a hoe from the tool shed as I sped toward the garden. I wanted to be casually hoeing when Marshall came out again. I had barely had time to get to the garden and get poised with my hoe when he came out again. This time he was carrying a small mahogany chest and he was just inching along toward the front gate. I hesitated a minute. Should I take my hoe to underline the idea that I just happened to be working in the garden, or should I drop it, which would seem more logical? I decided to drop it, then walked quickly up front to the walk. Marshall was making slow progress, staggering under the bulky load. I cleared my throat. "Uh, do you need some help?"

He jumped, but he didn't loosen his grip. He slowly and carefully put the chest down on the walk and dusted his palms together. "It's not particularly heavy," he said. "Just kind of hard to get a grip on."

"I just happened to be out working in the garden," I said as he knelt down to secure another grip, "and I couldn't help noticing that you've been . . . uh . . . carrying this furniture and the thing is, I just sort of wondered what you were doing with it, if you see what I mean." I cleared my throat uneasily. I felt pretty dumb, actually.

Marshall didn't look angry, though. He seemed almost eager to explain. "I'm taking them home to fix them up," he said. "Come over here and look at this."

Was it possible Marshall intended to get me close, sock me, then run? I wondered nervously. I wished that I had brought the hoe along in case I needed to defend myself. But when I did draw near, he only showed me a loose handle on the drawer.

"See this?" he said. "This is the sort of thing that needs fixing. And notice these worm holes?" They were very small, but when he pointed them out to me, I did see them.

"Goodness," I said. "That thing has problems."

"When I get it fixed up, it'll look like new," he said. "You should see the Windsor chair I fixed up last week. Looks like it just came out of the store."

"Amazing," I said. I was surprised to see there were faint red spots in Marshall's cheeks. He was actually excited about this furniture repair stuff. "That'll be a nice surprise for Miss Addie," I said.

"Yes," he said. "Won't it?"

As I walked back to the garden to retrieve my hoe, I thought that maybe this was just the sort of wholesome interest that was needed to keep Marshall out of mischief. I was sure it was good for him to be excited about something for a change. It was funny, I thought, how Marshall was wearing a sports coat and tie. Most people would move furniture in old clothes. Not him. But instead of that making him look great, the way you would think, it just made him look unsure of himself, as if he were afraid of what people would think of him in old clothes. It didn't seem fair, when I thought about it, that as much as Marshall worked at it he could never be as attractive as Kel was without even trying.

Suddenly I was startled by Kel's voice. "What are you looking so serious about?" he called from the fence.

"Life," I said. "I'm thinking deep philosophical thoughts."

"Well, don't tell me about it," he said. "How are your radishes coming along?"

"Nicely," I said, picking up the hoe and going over to the fence to meet him. "By the way, I just found out what Marshall is doing with that furniture he's taking out."

Kel raised an eyebrow.

"He's fixing it," I said. "He showed me the things that were wrong with this chest he took out today. He says he's going to fix it up as good as new."

"Oh?" said Kel.

"You act as if you don't believe him," I said.

"I'm not sure I do," said Kel. He looked off toward Miss Addie's house. "He's up to something, Corrie," he said. "We just have to find out what it is."

When I got back into my house and cleaned all the dirt off of me, I realized that what with all the work I had been doing in the garden I was outside so much I was getting the same sort of tan that Kel kept year 'round. A brunette would have sneered at it, but still it was a tan, and I was very impressed with myself for having a tan in April. Also, I could see that my hair had got a few platinum streaks in it. That was a nice change from the swimming season, when my hair got platinum streaks but they were always tinted faintly green from chlorine. If it weren't for the dirt under my fingernails, I thought, I could almost pass for a femme fatale, so why didn't it ever seem to occur to Kel to ask me out? I had already told him there was nothing between Marshall and me. It was beginning to look as if I just wasn't his type, and no amount of propinquity or platinum streaks was going to make him interested in me. On top of that, even Mason, who was clearly bonkers about me, hadn't asked me out.

"I don't understand it," I said later to Terri. "Mason has been looking google-eyed at me all year, but he's never even asked me out to a movie."

"I expect he's intimidated," said Terri. "He probably thinks you're so good-looking and smart you would just sneer at him."

"But I'm always so nice to him," I said. "Didn't you hear how I carried on about his brownies in home ec?"

"He probably thinks its sheer charity," said Terri cheerfully. "Probably thinks you just throw him a few crumbs of praise out of pity. What's this interest in Mason all of a sudden?"

"It's obviously hopeless with Kel," I said, "and I'm getting tired of sitting at home. I could stand having a little attention from a boy. It would cheer me up."

"I know what you mean," said Terri gloomily. Since her thing with Eric had fizzled, she had had a lot of free time too. "You ought to take up with Otis," she said with a sudden return to her usual good spirits. "There's a boy who isn't easily intimidated."

I groaned at the thought. "Well, one thing's going okay, anyway," I said, trying to look on the bright side. "Marshall brought back that chair he took out of Miss

Addie's house. He came back with it while I was outside this afternoon."

"That's good."

"Yup, I guess so," I said.

"But it would be nice, maybe, to have another mystery?" suggested Terri.

I admitted that it did appear I had developed a slight taste for excitement. My life seemed flat and stale these days. I was glad that Marshall had turned out just to be doing a favor for Miss Addie, but I had to admit I was a teensie bit disappointed too.

8

One afternoon I was out working in the garden when I realized that Marshall's station wagon had driven up in front of Miss Addie's house again. I jumped up and trotted toward the front yard. I got to the gate just as he was unloading the small chest from the back of the wagon. Marshall had done wonders with it. Before it had been sort of dull, but now it was sparkling in the sunlight, as bright as fresh lacquer. The wood was gleaming. "Goodness, Marshall," I said. "That's amazing. Why, it looks like new!"

He blinked. I held the gate open for him as he came through. I noticed as he passed that there weren't even any worm holes in it anymore. I guessed he must have filled them in with some kind of special putty and refinished the whole thing. It must have taken him hours and hours. I remembered very well the time Mom had refinished a chair. The whole time she kept saying, "How satisfying to see it coming along," and, "What fun!" But the comments had struck me as even more hollow than usual. She had stood bent over the chair for hours, scrubbing it with steel wool and inhaling the fumes from stripping solution. I kept being surprised she didn't pass out. If Marshall had been doing that, he must have a lot more determination than I had ever given him credit for. I followed him up the walk as he staggered along with the chest. "The difference really is amazing, Marshall," I said. "Did you do it yourself?"

He put it down to get a firm grip before going up the steps, blinking rapidly. "Pretty much," he said.

When I looked at those dead-fish eyes of his I couldn't think of anything else to say, so I walked on back to my garden. It certainly seemed to me that this closed the case. Now I had seen with my own eyes that Marshall was actually fixing up the furniture instead of stealing it.

Soon I was busy again with my harvesting. It had gotten to be time for me to present my garden project in home economics and I was picking the vegetables for the basket I was going to take in the next day. Some things hadn't lived up to the promises of the seed catalogue and some of them the bugs had feasted on. Others had fallen victim to Marshall's nighttime stomping. But even so, there was more than enough to fill my big basket. Particularly lettuce. I had an awful lot of lettuce.

I took all the vegetables inside and washed them off in the kitchen sink, being careful not to bruise their leaves. I wanted them to make a good appearance in class. I shook the water out of them and began arranging them on paper towels to dry. "Do you realize this is the first truly practical achievement I have ever accomplished?" I said to Mom. "I mean, I may not be able to sew a dress or cook a meal, but it's nice to know that if I were ever marooned on a desert island or something I would know how to grow my own food. I wonder how long a person could survive eating lettuce?"

Before I left for school the next morning I arranged the vegetables carefully in a big basket with a handle, cunningly fixing them so it didn't look like *quite* so much lettuce. I sprinkled a few drops of water over them to keep them fresh and wrapped plastic wrap tenderly around them.

Mom let me drive her car to school again, and I drove straight up to the school entrance and took it all inside. I didn't want to take the chance of anything happening to my project at this stage. In the home ec room, Mrs. Johnson was at a sewing machine sorting buttons into little boxes. When she heard me coming in, she looked up. "My goodness gracious, Corrie," she said. "Is this your project?"

I was pleased to see that she already looked impressed. "I just wanted to be sure nothing happens to it before class," I explained. "Getting this far with it hasn't been easy."

She smiled. "I'll take good care of it," she said.

Even so, I was relieved when third period came and I walked into the classroom to find my project notebook and my basket of vegetables still there. When everyone was settled, Mrs. Johnson rose. "Class, today we begin the presentation of our special projects. Corrie," she said, "why don't we start with you?"

I didn't even mind being the first to be called on. That's how well prepared I was. I went up to the front of the class to stand by my basket and began my presentation. Mrs. Johnson was clearly impressed by it. As I handed her my notebook at the end, she said, "I can see that you put a great deal of thought and work into this, Corrie."

I passed Kel as I went back to my seat and he gave me a knowing grin. Then Mrs. Johnson called on Melanie Hicks. Melanie stood up looking slightly uneasy. I saw that she was holding an aluminum pan. "My project is no-bake fudge," she said gamely. As Melanie explained how she had stirred chocolate flavoring into confectioner's sugar, Mrs. Johnson's face settled into lines of displeasure. I gave a happy little sigh. It was blissful to know that for once that look wasn't intended for me.

After class, Kel congratulated me. "Mrs. J. was completely wowed," he said. "Anybody could see that."

"I hope so," I said. "By the way, Marshall brought back the chest he took out the other day. It looked like new. He must have completely refinished it."

"Maybe I've had him all wrong," Kel said.

I looked at him closely to see if he was putting me on, but his blue eyes were guileless. He seemed to have actually stopped being suspicious of Marshall.

"What's the matter?" he said. "Why are you looking at me like that?"

"I don't know," I said. "I think the problem is that in spite of everything I still feel that Marshall is up to something. I know it doesn't make any sense."

Kel laughed. I was annoyed at him for laughing, but at the same time I wished he would put his arms around me and tell me not to be angry. I don't pretend any of that made any sense, but it probably had something to do with Kel being the most attractive boy I had ever known . . . and the most infuriating one. "You just need to figure out what he's up to then," he said.

"I think I will," I said.

To my pleasure he looked uneasy. "Now don't go doing anything dangerous, Corrie," he said. "I mean, don't go following him around and spying on him and dumb things like that."

Every word he said just made me madder. I didn't say anything.

"What are you going to do?" he asked.

"I'll be careful," I said. "Don't worry about me."

It gave me great pleasure to realize that as I strode away he was looking after me anxiously. I would have felt even better if I had had the slightest idea of how I was going to carry out my threat to find out what Marshall was up to.

I talked to Terri about it that evening when I was at her house. "I'd love to show him," I said hotly. "He's grabbed all the exciting stuff up till now, and he feels so smart. I'd love to be one up on him for a change."

"But Corrie," Terri protested, "this isn't your thing. You aren't the detective type. You aren't cut out for action."

"You shouldn't be so quick to pigeonhole people," I

said sharply. "Just because I've never done that sort of thing before doesn't mean I can't do it."

"Be reasonable," said Terri. "If you go around spying on Marshall, he's likely to haul off and bop you one. What would you do then? I know! Maybe you could pretend to like him and then draw him out or something. That would be better."

I gave her a black look. "Terri, Marshall knows that I know he stomped on my seedlings. Also, he has got to know that I suspected him of stealing Miss Addie's furniture. What makes you think he is feebleminded enough to believe that after all that I *like* him?" I could see that these details had temporarily slipped Terri's mind. "Besides," I said, "no power on earth could get me to go out with Marshall again, even to be one up on Kel." I paced the floor restlessly. "Oh, why can't Kel see me as a real person? All I am to him is somebody who stands by and applauds while he does his razzle-dazzle detective work. I'll show him!"

After I got back home and cooled off some though, I realized that unfortunately there was a little bit of truth in what Terri had said about me. The truth was I was not cut out for action. Also, I was more than a little bit of a scaredy-cat. The idea of sneaking into Marshall's house, for example, and searching his room didn't appeal to me at all. And as far as hopping into Mom's car and following him the next time the station wagon left with a piece of furniture, well, it looked easy enough on TV, but when you got right down to it, Marshall would have spotted Mom's little green Plymouth in a minute.

Somehow, I felt I should be able to figure out what

Marshall was up to if only I put my mind to it. After all, people might call me a marshmallow heart and accuse me of not being suspicious and not being cut out for action, but nobody had ever accused me of being dumb. Back in my room, I sat down at my window, leaned an elbow on the sill, and stared out at Miss Addie's gate while I thought. I remembered that old joke about the man who kept leaving the factory every day with an empty wheelbarrow and nobody could ever figure out what it was he was stealing, until years later he confessed it was wheelbarrows. Was this something like that? Was the furniture some kind of blind? Was the real thing he was after inside the furniture? That would make sense with the chest. I hadn't opened the drawers after all. But the theory didn't fit the chair. Next I considered "The Purloined Letter," the story by Poe. In that story everybody is looking for a stolen letter but no one looks in the most obvious place, the desk. Was this like that? Was what was going on so obvious I was missing it?

I was getting nowhere. Then I heard Mom's voice downstairs. "Corrie? Tim? I'm home," she called. I went downstairs. Mom was standing proudly next to one of the yuckiest-looking chairs I had ever seen. It looked like something you would find in the Seven Dwarfs' cottage, only rattier. Dad appeared and regarded it with bemusement. "Good grief, Margaret," he said, "is that it?"

"Yes," said Mom, her face glowing. "My very first antique. Isn't it fascinating?"

Dad walked around it, examining it dubiously. "I guess you're going to fix it up," he said.

"Oh, no," said Mom. "That would destroy its charm. This isn't an ordinary chair, you know."

"Yuck," said Tim.

Mom stood protectively by the chair. "The nice thing about it isn't its beauty but its history," she said. "You just haven't learned how to appreciate the character of the piece, the patina of age."

"Evidently," said Dad.

Mom set out to educate us. "Of course, I can't afford a really fine piece. This is a primitive. But there are interesting things about it. Look at this—see this worn-down place on the back?"

The whole thing was so worn it was hard to see at first what she meant, but at last I made out a large worn area; it looked as if the chair had been laid on its back and dragged behind a car.

"You see," said Mom enthusiastically. "It's probably been laid on its back and pushed around by a child learning to walk."

"You mean that's what they used before walkers?" said Tim, looking a little interested.

"Exactly," said Mom.

"Obviously they picked the ugliest chair in the house for it," said Dad.

Mom ignored him. "And see here? The knife marks? You can see that this was handmade. It isn't exactly elegant, but I think it has a certain grace and originality."

My mind was working so fast that I hadn't said a word up till now, but finally I asked, "Where did you learn all this stuff, Mom?"

"The antique dealer helped me out some," said Mom, "but I really got my interest in it from Miss Bertha. I suppose you children didn't realize it, but she was a great collector of antiques. She was fascinated with old furniture. Of course, she collected fine pieces. I couldn't afford anything like that, but sometimes she used to come over, have a cup of coffee, and share her philosophy. I learned a lot from her. Finally, I decided to take the plunge and buy something myself. Well, Corrie, you haven't said anything about the chair. What do you think of it?"

"I think it's the most interesting thing I've seen in ages," I said warmly.

Mom looked pleased.

"Mom," I asked, "what do people do if they like old-fashioned-looking furniture but they want it to look all new and shiny?"

"Why, they buy reproductions, of course. But that way you don't get a piece with any history. They're just copies of the real thing."

"But they're a lot cheaper, right?"

"Yes, but to my mind they're not as attractive as the mellow-looking genuine article." She looked at the yucky chair affectionately. "I had no idea you were developing an interest in furniture, Corrie," she said.

"Oh, I'm *very* interested," I said. I couldn't wait to get to Kel and tell him what I had figured out. Marshall must be replacing Miss Bertha's valuable antiques with shiny new copies. No wonder they looked like new. They *were* new. He was probably counting on the fact that her sister didn't care about furniture. Miss Addie hadn't actually lived in the house very long and wouldn't be likely to notice any substitutions he made. Also she wasn't the sort of person who went around the room running her finger over the furniture and checking it for scratches. To her a chair was just something you sat on.

"Where are you going, Corrie?" Mom asked. "I'm just about to put dinner on. I've got a casserole in the oven."

"Just next door, Mom. I won't be but a minute." I dashed out before she could ask any more questions.

To get to Kel's front door I had to pick my way through a forest of dirt bikes and two motorcycles. Over in the driveway enough cars and trucks were parked to stock a rental fleet. The Reids were never short of transportation, anyway. As I went up to ring the doorbell I saw that the heavy wooden door already bore a number of scars I didn't recollect from the Harrison's time. It looked as if a bike chain had been scraped across it, and there was another spot that looked as if it had been kicked by somebody wearing football cleats. I rang the doorbell. Crashing noises approaching the door told me that the bell had been heard. The door was flung open and Jason stood there, legs spread apart as if he were defending the home castle from invaders. He looked at me with cold blue eyes. Good grief, I thought. That stare must be hereditary. Imagine what breakfast must be like in that family with all of them zapping each other with those eyes. "Is Kel home?" I asked.

"Nope," he said. Then he turned to shout intelligence to those within. "It's a girl," he yelled. "Tim's sister."

I thought I heard somebody at the top of the stairs say, "Oh, phooey."

Mrs. Reid came bustling into the foyer, anxiously drying her hands on her apron. "That's no way to receive guests, Jason," she said. "Do come in, dear."

"That's okay, Mrs. Reid," I said quickly. "I can't stay. Mom's putting dinner on. Would you just tell Kel that I'm trying to reach him, please?"

"Of course," she said. "He's having dinner out tonight, but I'll make a note to tell him when he gets in."

I managed to smile as I left, but I thought, "Dinner out? With whom?" As I walked back to my house I found myself thinking that there was no rush to tell Kel. I needed to work out all the details first. I didn't have any proof, after all.

With all that was going on in my mind, it was hard for me to concentrate on making conversation at the dinner table that night. I was too busy thinking about Kel and his unknown dinner partner and Marshall and the stolen furniture. I knew now the reason Marshall had stomped on my seedlings. He probably didn't like the garden because with me working on it every day, Miss Addie's house was always being watched. He must have thought that if I got discouraged and gave up on my garden he could carry out furniture with nobody noticing. Maybe in the beginning he hadn't even planned to go to the trouble of getting replacements for the stolen pieces. He must have tried everything he knew to get me to give up the garden before he settled on the alternate plan of pretending to be refinishing pieces while actually he was replacing them with inferior copies.

"Corrie," Dad said, "this is the third time I've asked you to pass the potatoes."

"Is anything wrong?" Mom asked.

I passed the potatoes. "No, everything's fine," I said. What I needed to do, I thought, was to get some proof that my deductions were right. I had to conduct some investigations.

Later that night, Kel phoned. "Mom said you came over to see me," he said. "What's up? Have you found out anything."

"I think so," I said. "But I want to check out my deductions some more before I tell you."

"You mean after all this you aren't even going to tell me?"

"That's right," I said. I waited for him to say that he'd been busy at dinner interviewing for a summer job or organizing a cub scout troop, but he didn't.

"Okay," he said bitterly. "If that's the way you feel about it." He hung up abruptly.

9

The next morning before school, Kel tracked me down in the hallway. He trapped me in a corner and leaned over me, glaring at me with his icy eyes. "Now look here, Corrie," he said. "I don't know what you're up to, but I don't like it. I never kept any secrets from you when we were tracking down the stomper, did I?"

Mary Ellen peered at us curiously as she passed. "Uh, hello, Corrie. Hi, Kel."

We scarcely noticed her. "I know," I said. "But you got all the glory from that. Now I want a little glory. This is my idea."

"You can have the glory, whatever you mean by that," Kel said. "Just tell me what's going on."

"I don't have any evidence yet," I said. "I've got to do some investigating."

The bell rang and I tried to scoot out from under his

arms, but just as I thought I was getting away he put his arm around me and walked along with me.

"Let go of me," I said.

"Tell me," he growled in my ear.

This was getting embarrassing. People were looking at us. "Okay," I said. "I'll tell you."

We stepped out of the traffic near the lockers and I told him all my suspicions.

"I think you've got it," he said excitedly. "That's got to be it."

"But we've got to find more evidence," I said.

"How are you going to do that?"

The tardy bell rang and the halls fell quiet. In the silence my whisper seemed to echo among the lockers. "I'm going downtown this afternoon to interview some antique dealers and see if I can find out anything," I said. "If I can find out, for example, that Miss Bertha actually did own an antique Windsor chair and a small mahogany chest, that would be good evidence."

"I'm going with you," he said.

"I don't think you would look convincing in an antique store," I said, looking pointedly at his boots. "Besides, one person seems less suspicious." I was determined to go by myself.

He grinned. "Okay, Corrie. It's your show. But you come over first thing and tell me what you've found out."

We took off running then through the empty halls to our home rooms. When I ran in the door Mrs. Ellis was finishing up calling the roll and everybody looked at me. I turned red, wondering how many people had noticed the scene with Kel in the hall. I hate being a public spectacle.

Of course, maybe I had pushed Kel a little, but he didn't have to come on so strong.

Sure enough, later as we were filing out of home room, Lisa Wentworth murmured, "What's going on with you and Kel? I would love it if he chased me around like that."

"Oh, nothing," I said faintly. "Nothing." She looked after me disbelievingly as I turned into my chemistry classroom.

After I got home from school I told Mom I thought I might go downtown and look through some antique shops. "What a great idea, Corrie," she said enthusiastically. "That's the best way to get a feel for antiques. Reading about them is never quite the same. Try Antiques 'n Stuff on Elm and Tenth. That's a good place to browse. If I were you I wouldn't go into Antique Nook across the street. I don't think Mr. Krantz likes young people."

I took Mom's car. I was lucky enough to get a parking space right in front of Antiques 'n Stuff. As I got out, I saw the other shop, Antique Nook, across the street. I supposed that was Mr. Krantz standing at the entrance with his arms folded. I hoped he didn't have any information I needed. He had the expression of a parole officer.

A bell on the door tinkled as I went in, and a slender young man smiled vaguely in my direction. He was dusting furniture with a handful of white cloth. Light filtered into the shop softly and picked up motes of dust in the air. Big stuffed animals sat here and there among the furniture. There was a panda in a rocking chair and a large kangaroo perched on a desk. I could see that this place had antiques, all right, but somehow it didn't look quite like Miss Bertha's speed to me.

"I'm Corrie Lindgren," I said. "My mother said she didn't think you'd mind if I browsed around and tried to find out a little about antiques."

"Browse away, darling," said the young man. "That's what we're here for. If you've got any questions, I'm right here."

I had lots of questions, but I couldn't figure out exactly how to ask them. I pretended to examine a nearby rocking chair for a minute. Then I spoke to the young man again. "An old lady who lived in our neighborhood used to collect antiques," I said. "I wonder if you knew her. Her name was Bertha Hodges."

"I don't think so," he said. "We get mostly the young marrieds in here. It's the ambience, I suppose."

I had never paid much attention to furniture before, but I had begun to realize that Antiques 'n Stuff did not carry the sort of thing Miss Bertha would have bought. The shop had some heavy pieces of furniture made of yellow-looking oak, and there were some rough-looking pieces like the chair Mom had bought, but the chair and small chest I had seen Marshall carrying out of Miss Addie's house had been completely different from these things— graceful looking and made of smooth, dark wood. Oh, dear, I thought. This was the wrong place, all right. It looked as if I was going to have to ask crabby Mr. Krantz some questions after all.

The bell tinkled again as I closed the door of Antiques 'n Stuff behind me. I took a deep breath and crossed the street, squaring my shoulders to confront the awesome Mr. Krantz. I began to wish I had let Kel come with me after all. Kel was never scared. As I approached the shop,

Mr. Krantz lowered one black eyebrow and raised the other. It was not a friendly expression. I decided it was best not to actually go into the shop. Something told me that a person like Mr. Krantz would probably be worried that I would break something. Another thing I realized was that Mr. Krantz was not the kind of person you could stand around and make casual conversation with. My approach would have to be direct.

"Uh, good afternoon," I said.

Mr. Krantz nodded coldly. His eyebrows settled down on the same level, but the new expression was no more reassuring. I took another deep breath. "I'm trying to find out something about the furniture bought by my neighbor, Bertha Hodges," I said. "Was she a customer of yours?"

His eyes narrowed. "Why do you want to know?" he said.

"I think some of Miss Hodges's furniture may be missing, and I want to find out if there's any way to find out exactly what she had so I can be sure."

He looked away and admitted grudgingly, "Miss Hodges bought some things from me."

Now I was getting somewhere. "A Windsor chair?" I asked excitedly. "A mahogany chest?"

"No," he said.

I felt discouraged. This detecting stuff was harder than it looked. "Isn't there any way I could find out what she owned?" I asked desperately.

"Her insurance company would know," said Mr. Krantz. "And she probably kept some record herself, since she was a serious collector."

"Thank you," I said, surprised. "That's very helpful."

He smiled, baring little teeth. As I made my way back to the car, I had a twinge of sympathy for any young paper boy who had to collect from Mr. Krantz or any little girl who tried to sell him Girl Scout cookies.

When I got home and drove into our driveway, I scarcely had time to get out of the car before Kel appeared. He must have been watching for me. "What did you find out?" he asked.

"Not much," I admitted. "Miss Bertha did buy antiques at a store here in town, but those two pieces I saw Marshall carrying out weren't bought there. The store owner said, though, that her insurance company would have a record and that she probably kept a record herself. When it comes right down to it, I don't have any evidence at all. Even if I could figure out what insurance company she used, there's no chance they would let me get at their records, that's for sure. All I can do now is alert Miss Addie to the problem when she comes home and let her take it from there." It occurred to me that there was no way, really, I could keep Marshall from walking off bit by bit with every stick of furniture in the house.

"I think we can do better than that," Kel said.

"How?"

"Wouldn't you like to know," he said, dancing out of my reach.

"Kel!" I said, exasperated.

He laughed. "Just wanted you to know how it feels," he said. "Actually, I'm going to need your help. I want you to draw me a diagram of Miss Bertha's house."

I looked around me anxiously. "You aren't thinking of breaking into her house, are you? That's against the law."

"I'm not going to break into anything," he said.

"That's a relief."

"That second-story window over the back porch is unlocked."

"Kel!" I said. "I think it's against the law to get in that way too. What if you're caught?"

"Then you can be my character witness," he said.

"You are *hopeless*," I exclaimed.

"Well, you wanted to know," he said. "Now just pretend I haven't told you."

"Ooo," I groaned, burying my face in my hands. "Please don't do this! It is so dumb."

"You'd better draw the diagram. If I don't know where things are I might stumble downstairs in the dark and break a leg."

I looked anxiously around me again; then we walked over to a flower bed in Kel's yard and I sketched out the layout of the house as I remembered it, drawing with a stick in the dirt. "Here is where her bedroom was," I said, "on the second floor. Now down on the ground floor, over here, was a sort of library where she wrote her checks and stuff. I remember that from when I was selling Girl Scout cookies. She would go in there to get the checkbook. Honestly, Kel, I don't think this is a good idea. I think we should call up Miss Addie, that's what we should do."

"But she trusts Marshall," Kel said, "or she wouldn't have hired him to look after the house. And we don't have

140

any evidence. For that matter, our guess could be dead wrong.''

''*My* guess,'' I corrected him.

He grinned. ''I'll be careful,'' he said.

I was on edge all that evening, but there was nothing I could do. I couldn't even keep an eye on what was going on because I couldn't see the unlocked window at the back of Miss Addie's house from my bedroom. I could see it from the kitchen, but if I sat glued to the kitchen window all night Mom and Dad would have been sure to ask questions.

All that evening I never stopped thinking about what Kel was up to, but our phone didn't ring and no police sirens sounded, so I hoped everything was going all right. Even so, the next morning when I saw Kel in the hall at school, I felt almost weak with relief. He hadn't fallen down the stairs after all. He spotted me and held his hand up over his head to give me the okay sign. He was grinning broadly.

The suspense weighing on me all day was so acute it was like a pain. That afternoon, as soon as the bus dropped me off at home, I ran into the backyard to look for signs of Kel. He always got home before me because he drove himself. He was stretched out on the bench with his eyes closed. Looking at him lying there, I could feel my exasperation with him dissolving. Whatever dumb thing he'd been up to, I was just glad he was back safely. His lashes were silky and black against his lightly tanned face and the air stirred his hair gently. ''Kel?'' I whispered.

He jumped up abruptly. I let out an undignified shriek and then I saw that he was laughing. I sat down at the foot of the bench. "What if I'd had a weak heart?" I said crossly. "Then where would you be?"

Now I saw he had been lying on a black notebook. With a quick intake of breath I reached for it. Kel sat down on the grass looking mightily pleased with himself. "I wanted to surprise you," he said.

I leafed through the book. "Try page six," he said. I turned to page six and found a description and a photograph of the mahogany chest. Miss Bertha had written in the date and place of purchase and what was known about the history of the piece and also what she'd paid for it. "Not cheap," I commented.

"Nope, and you'll notice she bought it twenty years ago. That's the only chest, but I couldn't tell from the way you described it which chair he got."

I looked carefully through the book and saw that there were several Windsor chairs. "I can't tell either," I said. "A chair is pretty much just a chair to me. It was one of these, but I don't know which one." I closed the book. "I can't believe this. It is simply unreal. I mean, here right in front of my eyes, Marshall was stripping Miss Addie's house. The nerve of it! And my seedlings! It's so creepy." I had a sudden qualm. "You didn't leave any fingerprints in there, did you? And what are we going to do with the notebook now that we've got it?"

"It's tricky, all right," Kel admitted. "I don't like to put it back in the house for fear Marshall might get at it. It's important evidence. And I don't like to admit that we've got it because of the way I had to get it. I think I'd better tell Dad about all this. He'll know what to do."

My stomach felt full of butterflies. I realized now that

the fun part was behind us. This had been a kind of game, really, stopping Marshall's stomping and finding evidence against him, but when Kel told Colonel Reid, it wouldn't be a game any longer. Then it would be real. I gulped. "I guess we have to," I said.

That night, after supper, Kel phoned. Again I wished I had a private phone in my room instead of having to take the call in the kitchen where Mom and Dad pretended not to be listening.

"Corrie, I told Dad," said Kel. "He's going to take the notebook down to our safe deposit box tomorrow. He wants to call Miss Hodges tonight. We're just going to explain the whole thing to her. Dad thinks she won't care how I got the book. We'll just deliver it into her hands and let her give it to the police. Less explaining to do that way."

I realized that Colonel Reid was probably right about Miss Addie not minding how Kel got the book. She was an unconventional sort of person. And the idea of letting Miss Addie present the record book to the police was a master stroke. I just hoped fervently that Kel hadn't left suspicious fingerprints in the house or anything.

"Dad needs her phone number," Kel went on.

"Oh, sure. We've got it." I put my hand over the receiver and turned toward Mom and Dad, who were sitting at the kitchen table pretending to drink coffee and read the evening newspapers. "Dad," I said, "Colonel Reid needs Miss Addie's phone number. You have it, don't you?"

Dad jumped up hastily. "Of course; let me get it. It's in my desk." In a minute he was back with it and handed it to me. "What's this all about, Corrie?" he said.

"I'll explain in a minute," I said. I read the phone number to Kel. "Let me know how it goes," I said.

"Sure," Kel said.

After I hung up, I told Mom and Dad everything. I was glad Tim was in his room doing homework. I didn't want him to spill everything all over the neighborhood and give Marshall time to hide the evidence. As I laid it all out for Mom and Dad, their eyes grew wider and wider. "Marshall's poor parents!" Mom exclaimed sympathetically. "How awful for them!"

I was dying to know how things went when Colonel Reid called Miss Addie, but Kel didn't call me back. The next morning I spotted him in the hall before our home room class and ran to catch up with him. "Why didn't you call me?" I said. "What happened?"

Kel looked around, took my hand, and led me into the locker alcove, away from the traffic. I noticed Mary Ellen peering curiously at us as she went by. "I couldn't call you back," he explained, "because it was so late when we finally got through to her. She told us to call the police and have all the locks on the doors changed." He grinned. "She also said to lock the window over the back porch."

I let out a sigh. "Then the police are on the case now?"

"I think Dad's talking to them right this minute," said Kel. "Now, we've got to remember to keep this absolutely hush-hush, because if the word gets out, Marshall will start trying to cover his tracks and that will just make it harder for the cops."

"Right," I said. But I knew it was going to be absolute agony to keep it from Terri.

10

I met Terri for lunch, as usual. As she unwrapped her sandwich, she said, "Mary Snodgrass told me you and Kel were whispering to each other near the lockers this morning."

"We were just talking," I said, avoiding her eyes.

"I know you two aren't having a romance," she said thoughtfully, "so it must be something about that business with Marshall. What's up?"

"Oh, nothing," I said, feeling my face grow warm.

"Hmm," said Terri. "It must be a really big breakthrough. Maybe you've finally got something on him. But, of course, if you don't trust your oldest and dearest friend . . ."

"It's not that I don't trust you," I whispered. "It's just that I promised Kel not to breathe a word about it to anybody."

"Aha!" said Terri. "So something *is* up."

"It's something serious, Terri," I said. "I can't say anything else."

She looked thoughtful and ate the rest of her bologna sandwich without saying a word. Naturally, she finished quickly. Then she got up to leave. "Just keep in mind," she said sweetly, "that your oldest and best friend is well known for her tremendous discretion." Then she was off, leaving me staring dismally at my fish fillet. The cafeteria had a way of coming up with things that made a bologna sandwich look positively delicious by comparison.

Suddenly Otis Boggs appeared and slid into Terri's seat. This is what I get, I thought gloomily, for driving away my best friend. I get Otis. He kept his hair cut quite short, but that could not completely conceal that he had been born with glossy black curls. He had a rather long face and long ears, and his brow bulged a little as if to suggest the brain underneath. He also had spectacular white teeth, but right now he wasn't smiling. He swallowed hard. "Corrie," he said, "I know that a lot of young men are infatuated with you, but I sincerely believe that none of them can truly appreciate you the way I can."

Somehow Otis had gotten an idea of my social life that was completely off the wall, but that wasn't what worried me. What worried me was that a cold feeling in my stomach told me he was about to ask me out. Worse: to my horror, I could detect signs that I was beginning to feel sorry for him. My mouth felt dry. My whole life flashed before my eyes.

"You must realize," he drawled, gaining confidence as he went on, "that I've always deeply admired your intelligence. Don't you see that we can understand each other better than anyone else? We're two of a kind. We should give it a chance. Will you . . ."

At that critical moment Kel suddenly slid into the seat next to me. From the way he appeared so abruptly, he might have been a genie. "Hi there, Otis," he said.

Otis's shoe-button eyes glistened with rage, but he controlled himself. "If you will excuse us, Reid," he drawled, "Corrie and I were engaged in an intimate conversation."

Kel raised his eyebrows a fraction. "Sorry. This won't take long. Corrie, can you go to the Spring Folly with me?"

"It sounds lovely," I breathed, feeling faint with relief.

"Good. Well, I've gotta get on to class," he said. "So long, Otis."

"Uh, I'd better be going too," I said hastily. "I don't want to be late to Mr. Hankin's class again. Nice talking to you, Otis." I had the vague impression that Otis's face was turning slightly purple as I left, but the wash of relief over me was so strong I hardly noticed anything else.

Outside the cafeteria, I caught up with Kel. "I'll never forget this, Kel," I said. "You saved my life. What a narrow squeak! You can count on me any time you want a favor. Want your boots polished? Your windows washed? Think of me. I'll never forget the way you got me out of that. Never."

"What are you talking about?" asked Kel.

"About you saving me from Otis," I said indignantly. "You saw that he was just going to ask me to the Spring

Folly, didn't you? You popped up in the nick of time to get me out of it."

"Does this mean you won't go to the Spring Folly with me?"

"You mean, you really *want* me to go with you?" I stumbled a little and Kel put his arm around me.

"I asked you, didn't I?" he said. "I swear, Corrie. I don't understand why that Otis Boggs is so crazy about your intelligence. Sometimes you act as if you don't have the brains of a turtle." He gave me a peck on the top of my head. Mary Snodgrass passed by just then, all wide-eyed, and said pointedly, "Hi there, Corrie."

"Hi, Mary," I said. I giggled. If Mary went around telling the whole school that Kel and I were a hot item now, I wouldn't care. I felt wonderful—warm and tingly, happy to be alive, the way you feel when you've gotten off a particularly ferocious ride at a fairground and put your feet on the solid ground. Not only had I escaped going to the dance with Otis, but I was actually going to get to go with Kel. To think how close I had come to saying I would go with Otis! Imagine having to listen all evening to him saying how smart we both were! I could see that Terri was right. I really did have a problem with this business of getting sucked into awful dates. But I was going to work on it. I was going to lick it. I would sit in front of a mirror and practice saying, "I'm sorry. I have to wash my hair that night," a thousand times until I got it right.

Now only one thing was bothering me. Could Otis have been right when he said we were two of a kind? "Tell me the truth, Kel," I said anxiously. "Do you think I'm like Otis?"

Kel grinned. "Would I take Otis to the Spring Folly?"

"No, honestly. I mean, do you think my personality is like Otis's? I want to know."

"No, Corrie, you are not like Otis. Nobody is like Otis. You can count on that."

After supper that night I went over to Terri's, swore her to secrecy, and told her everything about Marshall and the antiques.

"Ooo," she said. "That sounds like big trouble for Marshall."

"I know," I said. "I really feel sorry for him." But my heart wasn't in it. I wasn't even very interested in Marshall right then. I just wanted to be on good terms with Terri again so I could tell her about how Kel had finally asked me out. "Guess what!" I said, not even bothering to try to work it subtly into the conversation. "Kel asked me to the Spring Folly!"

"Ooo, terrific!" said Terri.

"And it was such a near thing," I explained. "Otis was right in the middle of asking me when Kel swooped down and asked me first."

"You don't mean you were going to say yes to Otis!"

"I don't know," I said doubtfully. "I hope I wasn't."

"Gee," said Terri, "if Kel asked you out . . . this could be the start of a big romance! After all, when you think about it, guys don't shovel dirt for hours to help out girls they don't care about. I should have suspected it all along."

Suddenly, instead of feeling good, I felt insecure. I remembered the time I had gone over to Kel's house and discovered that he was having dinner out. For all I knew there might be another girl in the picture somewhere. Or if there wasn't, there might be soon. What I realized was that I liked having Kel around. I got a kick out of talking to him over the back fence. It had been fun working on the mystery with him. There was something so nice and solid about a friendship, so reliable. I wasn't sure I was completely happy about the idea of moving onto the slippery ground of romance. "What if Kel never asks me out again?" I said anxiously. "What if after this he starts avoiding me? What if this means the end of a perfectly good friendship?"

"What are you trying to do?" said Terri. "Squeeze all the misery out of this date that you can? If it makes you feel better, don't think of it as a possible romance. Think of it as advanced friendship."

I liked that. Advanced friendship. It sounded very solid. "You're right, Terri. You're absolutely right," I said. "That's what I should do." I felt better already. I was lucky to have a friend like Terri. I only wished I could wave a magic wand and make her as happy as I was.

For the Spring Folly I wore the same dress I had worn to the Christmas party. My savings account was too flat to think of doing anything else. But this time I got Mom to put my hair up on top of my head and weave tiny silk flowers into it. I figured that would give the dress more of a springtime look. I guess it worked out all right, because when Kel came to pick me up, he pursed his lips and gave a low whistle.

I was relieved to find that Kel had managed to wangle the Mazda for the evening because I knew the silk flowers wouldn't have survived if I had had to ride on one of the motorcycles or in the Jeep. When we drove off, the faint light from the dashboard reflecting on Kel's straight nose, I felt I could have looked at him all day. I just really, really liked him.

"Did you know Marshall's parents have hired a bigwig lawyer?" he said.

"No!"

"You could be called as a witness if the case comes to trial."

"You're kidding me," I said, beginning to feel sick.

"Well, think about it," he said. "You were the one who saw the antiques being carried out and the copies brought in."

"A minute ago, you said 'if the case comes to trial,'" I said, grasping at straws. "Do you think it might not?"

"You've heard of plea bargaining, haven't you?" said Kel. "What I figure is that the police might lower the charge against him if he agrees to plead guilty to something else. I don't know much about how it works."

It sounded good to me. Anything to keep me off the witness stand. I had seen all that on Perry Mason reruns, and it looked awful. I could just see me trying to testify on what the furniture looked like when I can hardly tell a Windsor chair from a milking stool. "I think this plea bargaining sounds great," I said. Kel grinned. "Honestly," I said, "don't you sometimes wish we'd never got into all this? I mean, look at all the trouble Marshall is in. And you know, I don't think Miss Addie would even have missed the antiques."

"You mean, let him get away with it?" Kel asked incredulously.

"It just seems too bad for everybody to be so miserable. Think of Marshall's poor parents."

"Marshall should have thought about that before he started a career in grand larceny," Kel said. "If he had gotten away with it, next thing we'd know he'd be into something else. This way he learns his lesson."

When I thought about it, I could see that we couldn't have let Marshall get away with it, but that didn't stop me from feeling sorry for him. "I wonder if he'll be at the dance," I said.

"Not a chance," said Kel. "He's got bigger things to worry about."

We pulled up in the parking lot back of the gym and got out. It was a cool spring night, not cold enough for the coat I had worn to the Christmas party, but cool enough for me to be glad when Kel put his arm around me. I had to pick my way carefully over the gravel of the parking lot to keep from demolishing my strappy sandals entirely.

Inside, most of the kids from school were already there dancing. The tumbling mats were rolled up in heaps in the corners, and the basketball hoops were strung with tissue-paper flowers. Some girls from Home Economics II were staffing the punch table, and at the other end of the gym a clump of teachers sat in folding chairs, casting friendly eyes over the dancers. It wasn't a romantic atmosphere, but I was happy anyway. There were so many people inside that it was a lot warmer in the gym than it had been in the parking lot.

Kel and I started to dance. It was a nice surprise to find that he could dance fine. We danced under a basketball hoop and brushed past the string of tissue-paper flowers.

Kel said, "You know something, Corrie? I've wanted to ask you out since the first minute I saw you."

The natural answer to that would have been, "Why didn't you?" But I didn't say anything. Kel was not the strong, silent, mysterious type, and I knew very well what he was about to tell me. I wasn't sure I wanted to hear it.

"And didn't you have your eye on me too?" he asked mischievously. We negotiated a tricky turn at the punch bowl and I looked away from him. "I mean, I saw you looking at me with the binoculars," he went on.

"What do you mean?" I said faintly.

"You know what a sharp eye I've got," he said.

"Vain about it too," I said.

"And vain about it," he admitted. "Anyway, the day we moved in I saw a flash of light from your front window and I made out that somebody was over there with binoculars, somebody with long, blond hair. Well, that couldn't be Tim, could it?"

I should have realized, I thought fretfully, that the sun might reflect off the lenses of the binoculars on such a bright day. I remembered how the glass in the gun cases had reflected the light. My dancing was shot to pieces. Marshall's conversation might have been boring, but at least he never made me get all out of step. "So I was curious," I admitted grudgingly. "New people moving in and all."

"But it kept up," said Kel. "I kept spotting those binoculars at the window. I couldn't figure it out, because people kept telling me that you couldn't stand me."

"People are wonderful," I said bitterly. I supposed Terri, who had only a few days ago been bragging about how discreet she was, had spread it all over the school. And probably the temptation to puncture Kel's self-assurance by letting him know that not everybody thought he was so great had been too much for a lot of people. I didn't say anything. I just tried to keep from stepping all over Kel's toes.

"Hey, are you mad at me?" he said.

"No," I said. The fact is, looking at somebody with binoculars is no crime, but it's a very embarrassing thing to get caught at.

"I just couldn't figure it out," he said. "I mean, I really took to you, but I couldn't figure out whether, if I asked you out, you would say yes or throw a clump of dirt at me."

"So you hung around a little to find out."

"Yep." He grinned. "You know, it's not just any old girl that I'd shovel dirt for."

I was beginning to feel better. So I looked silly. It didn't seem to have put Kel off anyway. "At first I thought I didn't like you," I admitted. "The way you looked at me, I felt as if you were just counting my faults."

"Not a bit," he said. "I was just taking it all in."

"Okay, well, anyway, I got used to it," I said.

"Gee, Corrie," he said, "that's the nicest thing anybody has ever said to me. You got used to me! Can I put that in my scrapbook and keep it?"

He was teasing me and the temptation to step on his toe was strong, but I realized that I wouldn't make much of a dent in those sturdy shoes, so I gave up the idea. When the music stopped we were conveniently near the punch bowl and gravitated toward it.

"Brownies," said Kel, eyeing the refreshment tray hungrily. "I love brownies."

I grabbed at his arm. "Marshall's here!" I whispered.

Marshall was standing next to the punch bowl holding a cup and sullenly surveying the dance floor. "Well, if it isn't Kel Reid," he said in a nasty tone.

To my relief, Kel took a step back, safely out of Marshall's reach, but this seemed to only make Marshall angrier. He drew his fist back and lunged at Kel. Kel stepped out of his way and was only grazed, but I could see he was angry. Luckily, at this point Mason and Joe grabbed Marshall. I could see some shuffling of chairs at the far end of the gym as the chaperones struggled to their feet fast in an effort to get to where things were falling apart down at our end. All at once a bunch of boys marched Marshall outside, and by the time the chaperones made it to our end of the gym, Marshall was gone and the boys were coming back in looking very pleased with themselves. Kel was still standing quietly beside me, looking a little white. "I feel like a perfect idiot with people having to pull Marshall off me," he said softly. "I wish I'd clobbered him."

I didn't say anything. I figured that after a second or two his sanity would return and he'd realize that it was better not to get into a brawl at a school dance. Chaperones were likely not to care who threw the first punch and might just suspend everybody in sight. I squeezed his hand a little and we started dancing again. Even in the midst of the crowd of kids, though, I felt conspicuous. People were talking about the fight, and every now and then somebody would look curiously at Kel and me. "What a mess," he said gloomily. "I kind of hate to act as if I'm having a good time after all that. It looks sort of heartless."

"Are you having a good time?"

He grinned. "Sure."

I smiled back at him, and he bent over and kissed me. I knew that probably somewhere nearby Mary Snodgrass was staring at us and pursing her lips, but I didn't even care.

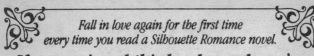

Fall in love again for the first time every time you read a Silhouette Romance novel.

If you enjoyed this book, and you're ready to be carried away by more tender romance...get 4 romance novels FREE when you become a Silhouette Romance home subscriber.

Act now and we'll send you four touching Silhouette Romance novels. They're our gift to introduce you to our convenient home subscription service. Every month, we'll send you six new Silhouette Romance books. Look them over for 15 days. If you keep them, pay just $11.70 for all six. Or return them at no charge.

We'll mail your books to you two full months *before they are available anywhere else.* Plus, with every shipment, you'll receive the Silhouette Books Newsletter absolutely free. *And Silhouette Romance is delivered free.*

Mail the coupon today to get your four free books—and more romance than you ever bargained for.

Silhouette Romance is a service mark and a registered trademark.

READERS' COMMENTS ON SILHOUETTE ROMANCES:

"I would like to congratulate you on the most wonderful books I've had the pleasure of reading. They are a tremendous joy to those of us who have yet to meet the man of our dreams. From reading your books I quite truly believe that he will some-day appear before me like a prince!"

—L.L.*, Hollandale, MS

"Your books are great, wholesome fiction, always with an upbeat, happy ending. Thank you."

—M.D., Massena, NY

"My boyfriend always teases me about Silhouette Books. He asks me, how's my love life and natu-rally I say terrific, but I tell him that there is always room for a little more romance from Sil-houette."

—F.N., Ontario, Canada

"I would like to sincerely express my gratitude to you and your staff for bringing the pleasure of your publications to my attention. Your books are well written, mature and very contemporary."

—D.D., Staten Island, NY

*names available on request